THE Vial OF Life

For your reading enjoyment! Marilyn Remus

MARILYN REMUS

ISBN 979-8-89130-689-9 (paperback)
ISBN 979-8-89130-690-5 (digital)

Christian Faith Publishing
832 Park Avenue
Meadville, PA 16335
www.christianfaithpublishing.com

Printed in the United States of America

Characters:
Allie Birks
Blake Winters
Mr. Freedman Carver II
Mr. Freedman Carver III
David
Ms. Wilheim
Jim Richards
Lenny Whiteall
Mexican Cartel (no names)
Oreo (the cat)

Incidentals:
Whispering Palms: retirement facility
Kensington: city near Arctic Circle
Time: month of September

CONTENTS

CHAPTER 1

Not Alicia

Her destination was the Arctic Circle. In the middle of winter. Alicia tried to sleep, but her eyes would not close, so she gave in and hypnotically stared into the darkness. The smell of breakfast drifted through the airplane informing her stomach it had not been fed for far too long. A perfectly groomed flight attendant with clear, wide-awake, perfectly lined eyes and a well-pressed outfit handed her a menu, breaking her staring marathon. Allie had been named Alicia after a great-great-aunt from somewhere on the family tree, and she was forever thankful her brothers immediately nicknamed her Allie.

Allie ordered scrambled eggs, bacon, hash brown potatoes, fruit, toast, orange juice, and coffee, inhaling the food so fast that it prompted the flight attendant to ask if she would like more. She finished eating long before everyone, thus winning the "who-can-eat-your-breakfast-fastest" contest. She amazingly found she could have eaten even more food, but she settled for a coffee refill.

Food and a trip to the restroom to fix what little makeup she wore gave Allie a mental "second wind" as she settled back into her first-class seat. She desperately needed to focus her thoughts, and she gave a silent thanks as she gently leaned her head against the coolness of the window. She concentrated on the solid, pure white-on-white clouds below, pretending she could walk on the stratospheric expanse of clouds where there would be no stress. No more running. And no questions. She would just be Allie Birks who owned a cat named

Oreo and lived quietly by herself in a Florida condo and worked at a retirement facility called Whispering Palms.

The plane shuddered as it encountered turbulent air, and with a jolt, reality set in. She went over what she had done. She followed instructions to rent a car and drive it to the Fort Lauderdale Airport, leaving it in the short-term parking section. Then she left the keys under the mat in the back seat. She bought a plane ticket and took the red-eye flight to Dallas, which touched down before the sun rose at 5:10 AM. Passengers drearily filed off the plane as if they were sleepwalking. The flight attendant gave everyone her best "Thank you for flying with Canada Air and have a nice day" speech, and Allie grumpily thought if someone told her to just be quiet, most passengers would cheer.

In Dallas the early morning darkness made it seem like the middle of the night. Allie checked her ticket and joined others as they blearily stared up at the arrival and departure screens. Adrenaline kept Allie moving forward until she found her way to the correct gate and boarded a 6:25 AM connecting flight to Seattle. As the flight took off, she took a moment to close her eyes, and the next thing she remembered was the smell of breakfast. Allie was not one to dwell on food, and friends often teased her that she was one of those people who "eat to live" and not one who "lived to eat," but today she marveled that she could hardly wait to eat yet another breakfast on this day.

After inhaling a second meal, Allie realized that the hours remaining gave her the perfect time to think. She took several dedicated deep breaths to give her mind permission to focus. Too late, she realized that was the wrong thing to do. She could feel fatigue claiming her body and her mind. She struggled to stop the descent into sleep, but her usually obedient mind defied her. Surrendering, she drifted away to the wonderful world of oblivion, and her last thought was that she desperately missed her feline roommate, Oreo. As she slept, Allie was completely unaware of another first-class passenger, who had changed his seat.

He positioned himself so he could watch her every move—on and off the plane.

CHAPTER 2

Whispering Palms

The five-story rectangular building stood back from the road as if it wanted to hide. Being painted an off-color gray with black trim did not help its appearance nor did an extensive overhang that dwarfed one side of the building. An archway had been added to the original structure, much to the disgust of the original architect, as it gave the impression of an overbite that somehow should have been corrected with braces.

Originally built as a luxury suite hotel, it was situated on the wrong side of the road on the outskirts of world-famous Palm Beach, Florida. Tourists vacationing in Florida wanted to be closer to the beach, and after several disastrous years, the hotel failed, was sold, and became a facility for elderly people who could no longer manage in their own homes. Families made the decision to place them there so they could have the convenient on-site services of nursing aids, housekeeping, maintenance, and three meals a day. This did not mean the sons and daughters of the seniors were mean or uncaring, but usually both husband and wife worked. They had children either living at home, or they supported them at college, and there was just no room or time to care for grandparents. They became known as the "sandwich generation" as they were "sandwiched" in between their parents, who lived much longer than expected, and the children they were still raising.

Most residents were moved in figuratively kicking and screaming as they felt they were quite capable of looking after themselves. In truth, most had to use some form of walker or a cane or a wheelchair to get around. A high percentage had some degree of short-term memory loss adding to their overall problems. Denial is a strong emotion, and it would take the seniors time to adjust to this new lifestyle.

Many of the seniors quickly learned to use the "guilt manipulation" emotion on their adult children, which could be compared to that of a three- or four-year-old temper tantrum. In the beginning, the ploy worked on their families, but as time passed, the seniors began to think of their new accommodations as home, and the guilt trips stopped.

Jim Richards walked up the stairs to the front lobby of Whispering Palms and felt his heart pounding. He had earned the new executive director position, and it became his responsibility to breathe new life into this building and the staff. The employees whom he would inherit were understaffed, overworked, and distrustful of a new administration. This was Jim's first executive director assignment, and he felt as if it was his first day as the school principal. He took a deep breath and walked through the front door to address his new world.

*****

As she began her shift, Gloria could not believe that one month had already passed since she began her new job as receptionist-assistant office manager at Whispering Palms. She noted the date on the calendar and thought, *They say time really flies by when you're having fun or getting old or both.* She had to smile at her own joke. Gloria was enjoying her new job, especially with the added new responsibilities of assistant office manager. *That will look so good on my resume*, she thought and smiled to herself.

She settled into opening her computer for the day's work when her peripheral vision told her someone was waiting at the front desk. She swiveled her chair to the left, put on her best receptionist's smile, and froze. What greeted her was the oddest sight so that she could not even say "good morning." In front of her stood two men who almost defied description.

Neither of the two men was tall, but the older of the two had apparently never mastered the art of dressing well. He was about thirty to forty pounds overweight, and as if to not acknowledge his huge potbelly, he always wore his suits at least one size too small. He wore old-style round glasses with thick lenses, but what Gloria could not stop looking at was his head, where an expensive, but very ill-fitting toupee perched. It almost appeared to be on sideways, and Gloria thought it made him appear as if he was tilting to the left.

The second man's body language made it obvious that he felt very uncomfortable, giving him the appearance that he seemed to pull himself inward. Gloria thought he looked tired and so probably appeared older than his actual age.

Feeling as if an eternity had passed in only a few heartbeats, Gloria stood and walked toward the two men when thankfully the taller of the odd couple spoke.

He kind of harrumphed and said, "My name is Mr. Freedman Carver the Second and he and I," he pointed to the shorter man with him, "have an appointment with Mr. Richards."

Gloria found her voice and said, "Of course, sir. I will check his appointment calendar."

"No need to look," he barked in a gravelly voice. "Our appointment is for nine o'clock sharp."

Gloria glanced at the clock on her desk, which showed it was barely past 8:30 AM, so she gave him her brightest smile and said, "Yes, sir. I will contact Mr. Richards. He is in the building. Would you care to wait in our presentation room? It is very comfortable. Perhaps you would like some coffee?"

He paused as if in deep thought and finally said, "No coffee, thank you, but we will both have some ice water."

Finally, the other man spoke and said, "Dad, I don't want any water."

Eager to ease the obvious tension between the two men, Gloria spoke. "Certainly, sir," and led them to the presentation room. She returned to her desk with her mind racing. *So, he is the father and the other man is his son*, she thought. That was quite unusual because usually the sons did the talking with the father in tow when families came to Whispering Palms looking to make living arrangements for their elders.

Gloria had grown accustomed to Cindy Hirsh, the marketing director, handling most tours; however, Mr. Carver had requested to see Jim, so she served them their ice water and then used the in-house beeper to alert Jim that his 9:00 AM appointment had arrived early.

Waiting for Jim to reply gave Gloria had a chance to view the two men, and she shifted her attention and studied the son. His face seemed worn and tired, and his brownish-blond and untrimmed long hair was tied in a ponytail. His face was covered by an unruly beard while he dressed worse than his father in clothes that could easily have come from a Goodwill store.

She sent another message to Jim, and she wanted to say "get down here right now," but instead, she typed, "9:00 AM apt. has arrived. Mr. Carver and son waiting to see you." She willed the message of "get down here right now" to him in mental telepathy, pretending it would work. She had a funny feeling about the Carver father and son couple, and she wanted to turn them over to Jim as soon as possible. She shook her head and turned back to her computer.

It certainly had started out to be an unusual day.

CHAPTER 3

A New Day

Jim checked his pager as he walked into the elevator on the fourth floor when Gloria, his new receptionist, messaged him that his 9:00 AM appointment had arrived. His watch showed it was just past 8:30 AM.

The elevator smoothly and obediently took its passenger to the first floor, giving Jim time to think. He continued to be inwardly amazed at his mixed feelings of balloon bursts of excitement, which immediately cascaded into sudden walls of pure fear. He had felt these emotions before when he realized he wanted to get married and then again when they bought their first house and then when they finally signed the mortgage papers. Each time it felt like a mental ping-pong match—the joy of wanting something so badly you could feel it in your gut and then becoming petrified you would get it. He even knew it owned a name. Adult responsibility. He thought he had matured and was past these emotions, but here it was again. He laughed out loud as his mind brought up the word *muffins*. His grandmother called children "muffins," and it became a family password to call and announce you were having yet another little muffin.

So once again, he was experiencing that fragile feeling of newness complete with muffins, and Jim decided he liked it. He was now the new executive director of a retirement facility, and he was beginning his third week, and so far, so good. Muffins and all. He smiled at this last thought as he stepped off the elevator into the lobby, only to see his receptionist, minus her usual composure.

He stopped in front of her, glanced at the two people in the room, and still smiling, he said, "Are we having a good day, Gloria?" It was an in-house joke they had developed when things moved faster than Gloria preferred.

"We certainly are," she said, "and…"

"And," he prompted.

"It is a father and his son, and, well, you just need to see them."

"Okay." Jim smiled at her and thought to himself, *How bad can this be?*

Jim went toward the presentation room, but then suddenly turned back to Gloria. Her reaction was immediate. "Jim! What are you doing? They are over there."

Jim gave a little chuckle at her stunned reaction. "I know, Gloria, but I just remembered that Allie Birks, our new activities director, is starting today, and will you handle things with her until I'm free?"

"Yessir, and I forgot to tell you that the father's name is," she glanced at her phone message pad, "Mr. Freedman Carver the Second."

Jim put on his serious look. 'So, then I have the 'Second' and the 'Third' in there?"

Gloria finally relaxed and fell into the conversational flow and repeated, nodding her head, "Yes. You have the Second and the Third." Jim turned away from her to stop a landslide of laughter from them both.

He went to the presentation room to welcome two men known as Freedman Carver II and Freedman Carver III.

CHAPTER 4

Team Players

Over at Allie's office, it was six o'clock, and she still worked in her office creating the schedule for the next month's activities when her phone rang. She answered it with her usual vocal energy. "Activities Department. This is Allie speaking."

"Hi, Allie. This is Jim Richards. Somehow, I just knew you would still be in your office. Don't you think it is time to go home?"

Allie smiled. Jim had left the Marketing Department at Gardens months ago, and she was glad to hear his voice. "Well, Mr. Richards. How are you and where are you, and yes, I should be going home." Allie playfully ran all her words into one sentence.

"I am just fine, thank you," he said, mocking a serious, professional tone. Lightening up, he said, "I wanted to touch base with you, Allie. Are things still the same at good old Gardens? He shortened the facility name as all the employees did. Villa Resort Gardens was just too much to have to say.

Allie carefully said, "By still the same, you mean…? "She always remained careful in her replies to everyone when it came to work. One never knew.

"That's the Allie I remember," Jim countered. "Stay firmly on the diplomatic side of the road." They both laughed, understanding the unspoken thought.

Jim got right to the point. "Allie, in answer to your 'where am I question?' I am the new executive director of Whispering Palms."

Jim tried to keep the pride out of his voice but was not successful. He had worked hard to get to this point in his career, and he became inwardly thrilled every time he said those words.

Allie immediately felt happy for Jim. "Jim, congratulations. I am so happy for you. You deserve it, and I know you will really do well in that position."

"Thanks, Allie." Jim knew she meant it. Allie was that way. "Listen, I would really like it if you could come down and take a look at our facility." Jim kept talking, so she could not interrupt. He knew he had to sell her on his idea. "It has so much to offer, and I have already hired Betty Baird for office manager, Gloria Bent as receptionist, and I think you knew Cindy Hirsh who was our head nurse. They are good team players, Allie, and I have an opening for an activities director, and I know that you would be perfect. It is a great opportunity, and I really hope you can come down and see what we have to offer."

Jim finally stopped talking, but he heard only silence from Allie. "Allie? Are you still there?" Jim waited.

"Oh, yes, hang on, Jim. I am just picking myself up from the floor."

Jim chuckled. Allie's sense of humor was notoriously well-known. Do you want me to call 911?" he teased.

Allie sounded breathless. "No, that will not be necessary. I have a cylinder of oxygen right here in my office. Jim, I did not expect that. I am so glad the other people are with you, but I am not really looking to change jobs, but thanks for thinking of me." Allie shook her head and tried to keep up with the fast-paced conversation. *Change jobs?* she thought. *Why would I do that?*

Jim continued to press her as he outlined the positives of his offer. He knew of the tremendous tension that had become a daily struggle for employees at Gardens since the new executive director had taken over. Knowing it would not be professionally fair if he mentioned that, he said, "Allie, that is often the perfect time to make a change. The staff already here are good, and they know the residents, and Betty, Cindy, and Gloria are fitting right in. Everyone is working well together, and it is a good team, Allie, and I need a great activities director who knows what they are doing, and that person is you."

Allie found her mind racing despite herself. A good team. She liked that. There certainly was not a team left at Gardens as so many employees had left because of management problems.

Jim saved his best for last. "Allie, financially I can offer you two thousand dollars over your present salary. Maybe more if you twist my arm." He paused. "Look, it is only four miles south of Gardens. Please just come down and look. That is all I ask."

Allie felt herself giving in. "Well, I could come and look, Jim, but you need to know that is all it would be. Just looking." *What harm could it do?* she thought. It would be interesting to see how other facilities worked, and she could say "hi" to Betty and Cindy and Gloria.

Jim breathed a sigh of relief. "Great! Tomorrow then. What time would be good for you?" Allie knew her work schedule by heart. "Let me see. The residents handle their own bridge time, and I could get away then, so how about 4:30 PM?"

"Perfect! Four thirty it is. I am really looking forward to seeing you, Allie. And thanks. You will not regret this," Jim said with confidence in his voice.

"Jim, remember I'm just looking."

"Right. Just looking." He chuckled. "Bye, Allie."

Allie slowly hung up the phone, and suddenly it felt as if the walls of the office were closing in on her, and she realized how tired she felt. A light supper with a glass of wine and her cat, Oreo, curled up beside her would be perfect. Next month's schedule would get finished tomorrow. *I will just go and look*, she thought as she closed the office door behind her.

She was already planning what she would wear.

CHAPTER 5

Whatever Means Necessary

The meeting took place in an office that by appearance alone would cause even the most high-priced lawyer to be left breathless at its grandeur. Only the most expensive furnishings graced the room. Walls stood covered with a rare Chinese silk paper of ivory coloring so delicate it appeared to be suspended in air rather than serving as a wall covering.

A tapestry of shimmering colors ranging from exquisitely gentle pastels to wild, bold swatches of deep burning red hung on the wall behind the desk, and the colors blended so effortlessly that it was impossible to tell where one color ended and the other began.

On the wall facing the tapestry hung an oil painting comfortably seated within a frame of carved wood intertwined with flecks of silver and gold. The overall effect of the room was like the inside of a church with high walls of stained-glass windows to allow the sunshine to seep deep within the quiet hush of the semi-darkened room.

The carpet was colored a few shades darker than the ivory walls and seemed to welcome the weight of a visitor, allowing no sound and giving one the feeling of floating across it rather than walking.

Soft complementary lighting came from insets deep within the ceiling at angles that seemed to defy identification. The ambience shown was neither too light nor too dark, giving the room a warm yet cool appearance of enveloping comfort. However, it was not a welcoming comfort, but more of a silent statement of comfort that only wealth can buy. One wall remained naked as if to remind the visitor that nothing was overdone.

And there sat the desk. It complemented but also totally commanded the room with no sharp lines or square corners anywhere. It gave the impression it could flow like an ocean wave with soft but demanding lines. It was a masterpiece of blended woods from trees that had lived many lifetimes, and uncountable layers of high-quality veneer gave a glow that spoke of the owner's wealth and power. It was more a piece of exquisite art than a desk.

Four well-dressed men in various shades of dark suits sat around this desk in soft, sleek black leather chairs that, at first appearance, looked comfortable but once seated, an immediate sense of not remaining too long could be felt. It was an odd feeling and had been quietly discussed between the men and never repeated in case it might be taken as a criticism instead of an observation.

It was wise to be early, as the meeting would begin exactly on time, and one must never anticipate what might be required. There was no talking. There was no background music. Each man sat quietly as if trained not to present any unnecessary movements. The sound of breathing was not even present, and it forced everyone to be very aware of the sound of their own heartbeats.

A door soundlessly opened, and the owner of the desk entered the room and immediately sat down. He did not acknowledge the men, nor did he look at them. He appeared to contemplate the sheen of his desk, and without looking up, he said, "So."

The man sitting on the far right of everyone spoke. "We have not found him yet, but we have some leads, and we are checking those now. We have his last sighting in Miami."

"Do we know if he has the vial?"

"We suspect he does. We found his hotel, and he seemed to have checked out sometime very early in the morning. Apparently, the night clerk slept through it and could only guess the time. We searched his room, found nothing, and so he must have it with him."

Another man spoke. "It seems that he has spent several weeks in a kind of rehab center just south of Miami called Whispering Palms. He is using the facility as a kind of hideaway home away from home.

We do not know if he needed their services, but it tells us why we could not locate him. We are working on the claim of confidentiality from Whispering Palms and should have the information by tomorrow."

There was a brief silence, and the owner of the desk said without looking up, "What about his family?"

A third man spoke. "We located his father. He lives alone in Texas, and it seems he flew out to Florida several days ago. We are checking all the hotels, so it should not be too long."

There was another brief silence, and the man behind the desk slowly looked up and spoke in measured tones. "I want all the information about the vial and what it can do. Use whatever means necessary. We will meet back here in forty-eight hours—same time." As everyone stood, the man behind the desk disappeared as quickly and quietly as he had arrived.

For all intents and purposes, the meeting appeared to be a legitimate professional, corporate-type meeting. It was, in fact, a secret gathering of men who worked for a high-level underground Mexican cartel. They were a handpicked international group whose recent assignment was to find an American scientist who had developed a serum capable of replenishing earth's much depleted soil. It could even overcome the ravages of a nuclear blast and fallout, and it was so complete that it made water totally unnecessary for immediate and sustained growth. It would easily feed a world's population under any adverse circumstances.

Had this American scientist been under the umbrella of his government, it would be extremely difficult to obtain his findings. Every country had layers of protection and secrecy regarding scientific discoveries. Countries did not trust each other. Governments maintained an internal force of skilled men and women given government permission to do anything and everything necessary to maintain top-level secret information. It was not well-known, but there also existed another force, within the United States, whose duty it was to watch their own countrymen as they dealt with the international people. No one trusted anyone, thus making it an incredibly dangerous and secretive field.

The immediate disappearance of the man left the four men standing. There was silence you could cut with a knife. No one moved. Their eyes revealed nothing as each man stared ahead in an unblinking frozen pose. Then, as if each man had heard a silent command, they moved as one. Silently.

They seemed to float as they moved toward the exit door, taking with them the command to "use whatever means necessary."

CHAPTER 6

A Good Sign

Allie parked her beloved red car she had nicknamed Princess in a secluded corner of the parking lot. The Lexus was not new, but it was paid for and was her special luxury. The burning Florida sun reflected off the shiny exterior in shards of reddish light. Allie felt safe inside her car, and often, when she was faced with having to venture into an unknown situation, she would sit in the vehicle, letting the protected feeling of being in a cocoon give her an inner calmness.

She sat in Princess and looked at the building. She was stalling for time to gather herself before she went in to her new position. She decided it scored about a five on a scale of ten for appearance except at night. She had driven by after speaking with Jim, and someone sometime had spun the creative idea to outline the building in small white lights giving it a sparkling, magical Cinderella look at night.

The building was called Whispering Palms Luxury Assisted-Living Facility. Allie's first visit to this building had been just over a month ago, when Allie told Jim Richards that she would agree to "look" at the facility. Allie and Jim had worked together at Villa Resort Gardens when a new corporate director created an atmosphere of unsettling management decisions. Allie watched employee morale plunge around her. She lost the best boss she had ever had, and in all, thirty employees including Jim either left on their own, decided to retire, or were outright fired. It had not been an easy time.

Allie inwardly felt that Helen, the present executive director of Gardens, managed the necessary changes poorly. It surprised her as she knew Helen and had expected far better results from her. She also knew that Helen had not been truthful in dealings with staff and residents; however, Allie had learned to weather management changes. It became a matter of working hard, not repeating rumors, and basically keeping your head down until the dust cleared, and hopefully, you and your job remained intact.

As she became the only person left in the Activities Department, residents were adamant that few, if any, changes were to be made in their daily schedules. The variety was endless. They enjoyed bingo, bridge, art classes, exercise, shopping, cruising, and a litany of other types of entertainment. If the corporate office heard of any complaints, they would immediately interfere, and no one wanted that to happen.

So it was that Allie worked long hours managing the Activities Department doing her "absent" bosses work as well as her own. The executive director had yet to hire someone to be her boss. Allie knew they were taking advantage of her work ethic; however, she still worked a seven-day week with long hours each day to hold the program together. This work pattern, long ago cemented by her mother and father, did not allow her to let a packed activity schedule slide. She tried not to think about her increasing fatigue, so she kept telling herself it would soon be over. She never imagined that "being over" would mean going to another job. The call from Jim could not have happened at a more strategic time. It is strange how twists and turns in life often do not allow you to see around the bend ahead.

Allie knew she should leave the comfort of her cocoon car Princess, but she had arrived at least thirty minutes early. The addictive smell from the rich cup of coffee she had brought convinced her to melt into the coziness of the car seat. Much like an athlete preparing their mental readiness, Allie had instinctively learned to manage new situations by giving her mind permission to wander on thoughts having nothing to do with the present. Then slowly, ever so slowly, she would bring into focus the new "moment" facing her.

In her mind the "moment" became a round, crystal-clear bubble with rainbow colors. She imagined the bubble surrounded and protected her with brightness and an inner glow. Allie was not aware this was a form of self-hypnosis, and over the years, it had always worked for her.

Allie had experienced a variety of occupations, excelling at all of them. At age nineteen, she had completed junior college with grades good enough to go further in education, but her true passion lay in theater. She had embraced two glorious years as a professional dancer until a severe foot injury forced her to limit her creativeness to only being able to choreograph. While she excelled as an excellent choreographer, even more than a dancer, she found that she became impatient to see more than the inside of a dark theater or a drafty rehearsal hall, especially when she could not perform.

She worked as a flight attendant until the hectic traveling schedule made her long for a job in one place. She decided on a position in the Medical Records Department of a hospital, quickly moving up to the corporate office as human resources manager.

On a visit to see her mother in Victoria, British Columbia, who was then living in an independent facility, Allie found an unknown joy in being with and reaching out to seniors and making them happy. She found hugs and gentle pats on the arm brought such happiness to those navigating the last years of their lives that she threw herself into learning how to handle activities for seniors.

That is how Allie became an assistant activities director at Villa Resort Gardens, which was a large facility with 172 apartments. The residents occupied either independent-living levels or assisted-living levels. Allie used her creative and administrative abilities to enhance the job, and the residents recognized how her talents made their lives easier, and they loved her for it.

She flourished in this atmosphere, choosing to remain as an assistant and eventually worked under four different activities directors. Turnover figures could be high in this service industry caused by the changes of management, not the talent of the activities director in charge. Allie watched and learned well.

She took a deep breath and knew she could not put off entering the building and her new job any longer. She had given her thirty-day notice at Villa resort Gardens, and this was her first day of work at Whispering Palms as their new activities director—a new title for Allie.

Jim had done an incredible job in showing her all the reasons why she should move forward in her career path. While she had been outwardly insistent that change was not in her agenda, she could not ignore the gut-level feelings that told her the time had arrived for change. With this new job at Whispering Palms, she would now oversee her own activities program.

Well, she thought, *I had better get in there and start earning the substantial raise that came with this new job*. As she walked toward the front lobby door, rays of sunlight fell across the threshold.

A good sign, she thought, as she walked into the next chapter of her life.

CHAPTER 7

Call Me Sir

Working as an independent scientist, he had different rules. He did not answer to a governing board or an employer, and so he worked as a free agent, so to speak. He had so many failures over the years that any government interest became virtually nil, and eventually he, and his work, went into obscurity. He was totally content with his hermit-like life, and many in the scientific community did not know of him or, if they did, thought he had either stopped his experiments or perhaps even died. He kept in contact with no one.

Whether it was intentional or an accident, this scientist finally developed a formula whose characteristics and properties had the ability to stimulate seeds so that they would produce the most prolific, germ-free growth. It worked for all plants of this planet and would make their size and quality twice as good as man had ever been able to develop. It could produce excellent growth even in the absence of water or sunlight. When ingredients of the serum were correctly integrated, they could be kept in vials for months before use and, if kept in an ordinary refrigerator freezer, would last for years.

Outlining the amount of terrain it would cover was easily determined by the amount and mixture of the formula. The vial would be placed on the edge of an area to be treated, and when the cork-like seal, much as in a wine bottle, was broken and removed and the serum was exposed to air, a bluish gel-like substance immediately bubbled out.

The same bubbling effect can be achieved by putting baking powder in a drain and then adding vinegar, but that is where the scientific comparison ends. The chemical reactions may look alike, but one cleans the drain pipes, while the other creates lush growth. Once the formula touched the ground, it held a random puddle shape and then seemingly disappeared, leaving a white powderlike footprint. What one could not see was that the mixture increased upon itself, sending out rootlike streams of liquid until it reached the desired coverage. It would then turn back upon itself in a soft, controlled wavelike motion and, reaching the point from where it started, would bind together and settle into a thin liquid layer. It did not matter if the soil was healthy, depleted totally of minerals, laced with gravel, or was complete sand. It could even overcome the ravaged soil that may have been at the site of a nuclear blast with radioactive fallout.

The serum was so complete it made water totally unnecessary to produce and sustain growth. It could feed a country or the world under any conditions. With the changing of earth's climate, the depletion of fresh water and increasing populations on a global level, when knowledge of its almost magical qualities became known, possession of this vial would be sought by many.

The American responsible for the birth of this scientific discovery was known as The Third, and he had a reputation for being erratic in his beliefs. He lived in solitude deep in a rainforest-like area of southern Georgia. For years no one had paid any attention to his ongoing experiments that seemed to fail again and again.

The inherited wealth of his family had always allowed him to live in comfort without any thought of expenses. He was not a materialistic soul, and in truth, he was like a virgin concerning money. It meant nothing to him. He lived for his work. He had tried, early in his career, to interest some government scientists he studied with at the University of Georgia in his work. However, with his constant failures came little or no response, and so he worked on his own certain that one day he would make his formula work.

Locals had long ago decided he was a harmless sort, and as years passed, he became the area's kind-of-crazy person who never socialized. He never hurt or offended anyone either, and so they left him alone. In some sense, they felt they should protect his privacy. The "Southern feeling" was that each man had a right to his own way. He was never aware of this, of course, as he kept plodding ahead with his experiments.

His only contact with the outside world was a slightly mentally handicapped male. In the South they would call him "slow," and he worked as a delivery boy for the area grocery store. Every two weeks he came faithfully for the food order and just as faithfully delivered it the same day.

As time passed, the two men developed an "understanding." It was not an actual friendship like most of us would experience, but they grew to accept each other, and passing time brought a strange level of trust. The scientist was a father figure only in the sense that he was older and very quiet, and the delivery boy brought out the elder's protective feelings for a young, obviously not-too-intellectually-endowed person.

Several months after they had settled into this biweekly schedule, they had a conversation of sorts. When asked what his name was, the boy replied, "I'm David."

"Just David?" replied The Third. "Yes. My name is David."

Neither were apparently blessed as great conversationalists, so this had been quite an occasion. "Thanks, Dave" was the reply.

The boy stood a little taller and said, "No. Not Dave. It is David." Silence hung in the air between them, and suddenly the scientist let out a great guffawing sound like a laugh. "Okay then. David it shall be."

David looked at the ground, shifted his weight back and forth a few times, and then said, "What's your name?"

Another silence while the elder apparently thought about his name. "David, you can call me Sir." David was immediately pleased with this knowledge and nodded his head and repeated, "Sir."

As David ran off repeating the new name to himself so he would not forget it, the older man watched him as he disappeared into the woods. Each filled a void in the life of the other without giving a thought to this very basic human need. Life and friendships can be exquisitely uncomplicated when we leave them alone to grow in their simplicity.

Finally came the breakthrough in his experiments. He had to be in contact with a lab to conduct a scientific double-blind experiment, so word of his success had seeped out to the scientific community. It seems he was now running from everyone, even his own government. He found it hard to trust anyone, and whoever found him first would have the options to control the earth's future and the power that went with it.

The scientist's name was Freedman Carver III, and he was now living and hiding at Whispering Palms.

CHAPTER 8

Good Grief

Allie awoke with a start having fallen asleep on the flight to Seattle. Her mind and body had taken the needed sleep it craved. She struggled to make sense of the fact that she was not in her bed with her contentedly purring cat, Oreo, by her side. She found herself sitting up in an airplane seat winging her way ever closer to Seattle. For a moment she thought she was dreaming. How could she be in an airplane? And then she felt the cool smoothness of the vial that hung around her neck, and the memories of the past weeks flooded her mind. Allie closed her eyes, and her mind drifted to the workplace that occupied so much of her time and energy. She loved her work, and the results showed from the happiness that the residents displayed to the excellent reviews Allie received from the Whispering Palms Corporate Office.

The families of today struggle to meet the expenses of mortgages and increasing cost of living expenses while both parents work to have two paychecks to meet these goals. They work hard to raise their children while still having their parents living into old age. The young families do not have the room in their homes to allow their parents to live with them, nor as both worked, could they be present to tend to their needs. The obvious answer becomes facilities like Whispering Palms where their parents could live in a place where they have the constant care they need.

Of course, Allie knew of the situations of her elderly charges not being able to live with their families. She thought of herself as the person in their lives who was there to offer them a happier time in their advanced ages. They made new friends, and they played games they could enjoy such as bingo and cards while feeling content and safe in their new living conditions.

At first, almost every elderly person fought being put in a facility such as Whispering Palms, and it pained their children who were only trying to make the best of difficult situations. Eventually, the parents found that their new homes at Whispering Palms were palatable and even pleasant, and they relaxed and blended into the routines set for them.

Most of them looked upon Allie with great fondness, treating her as their adopted daughter. They would tell their children how much they cared for her. Of course, this was hurtful to the adult children, but Allie's open and honest personality and willingness to do whatever the families wished for their parents showed them that Allie was a welcome addition to the lives of both the elderly parents and their adult children.

The corporations that offer the facilities to house the elderly are aware of how valuable employees like Allie are to the success of their ventures. It's probable that Allie did not realize her value as she could have certainly required a higher salary. Managers like Jim knew that employees who possessed qualities like Allie are few and far between, and he was constantly making certain that Allie was happy working at Whispering Palms. He valued Allie as a person, and he was truly upset with the disappearance of his prize employee.

Good grief, she thought, and she allowed herself to smile because the words *good grief* would always remind her that Charlie Brown would say them in his frustrated dealings with life and Lucy in the well-known and beloved comic strip *Peanuts*.

Allie shook her head to wake herself up from her deep sleep and said the words "Good grief" out loud, but then her smile disappeared. She was in an airplane heading toward Seattle, Washington, running from unknown dangers. She sat very still. It really was not funny. She could very possibly be in great danger, and yet she had chosen the unbelievable task of leaving her warm and safe home and working in Florida and flying from the Sunshine State to an address in the Arctic Circle.

"Good grief" did not begin to cover it.

CHAPTER 9

What Had He Done?

The two men glared at each other. Finally, one man spoke. It was The Third, and he raised his voice as he yelled, "You should not have come. I did not need you to come. I have been living my life just fine without you. I do not want to live here, and you need to go back to Texas." Exhausted with the emotion of saying so many words, he collapsed into an overstuffed chair. There was a loud silence, and finally the other man spoke.

"Do not yell at me. I am your father, and I do not need that tone of voice, so just stop yelling. It does not help."

"I'm not yelling," The Third yelled. Then he heard himself and had to admit that he was yelling. He took a long, deep breath, exhaled loudly, and shook his head. "Yes, I did yell, and you are right. It does not help the situation, but it does make me feel better," said The Third as he measured his words in tone and spacing.

The Second nodded and released a lone chuckle from deep in his voice box. The Third matched The Second's one chuckle and added more sounds of laughter, and then The Third introduced a literal guffaw, which became a loud and long laugh. Soon both father and son were instantly convulsed in gigantic belly laughs as the two men found they had to laugh, or they would dissolve into the act of crying.

Finally, after they had laughed themselves into exhaustion, The Second said, "Oh, son. I moved you into Whispering Palms so that you would not have to deal with the outside world, and yet you have found a way to screw things up. What have you done?"

The two men, the father and the son, sat in silence as the question hung in the air. Indeed. What had he done?

CHAPTER 10

Mention My Name

The man sat only a few feet away from Allie in the airplane, but he did his best to blend into the upholstery of the seat. He appeared to be lost in reading his newspaper. It was imperative that he did not allow Allie to become aware that he was following her. He decided it was time to test to see if she was suspicious of his presence, and so he slowly lowered his newspaper and spoke to no one in particular.

"I don't know why I do this," he said loudly enough for Allie to have heard him.

She remained silent.

He rustled the newspaper and began to fold it into sections. "Honestly," he said, visibly shaking his head, "it's a crime."

Allie took the bait and said, "What is a crime?" It was not an interested reply, but more of a human reaction to a comment that seemingly needed to be addressed.

He looked at Allie and shook his head. "If I see one more story about people being driven out of their homes because the landlord wants to raise the rent and he needs to have them leave so he can charge new renters more money, I'll end up cancelling my newspaper subscription."

By this time Allie was looking at him, and so he kept talking. "Sorry. I did not mean to bother you. It is just that my niece is having to deal with this same situation, and it makes me so angry. It all seems so unfair."

Allie felt she should show some understanding of his comments as he was quite upset, so she said, "Sorry to hear that your niece is having this problem." It was all he needed.

"Oh no, I am so sorry," he said with obvious enthusiasm, and he pushed the conversation further. "I do apologize for my outburst. It is just that I feel protective of her, and I do not want my niece to have to give in to a landlord who only cares about increasing the rent."

"That's all right," said Allie. I rent the apartment I live in, and I really understand how you feel. Your niece is very lucky to have such a caring uncle."

"Well, thank you. But I should not have reacted so strongly just now. It is just that I do not want to see her struggle."

"She's lucky that you're in her corner," said Allie. "Not everyone has family that care."

"Thank you for understanding, and again, I do apologize for my outburst. Is your apartment in Seattle?" and he smiled and relaxed back into his seat as he continued their conversation.

"No," Allie said, "I live in Miami."

"Miami?" he said with total surprise dripping in his tone. "Good heavens. Why are you on your way to Seattle?"

Allie suddenly realized that she did not want to pursue this conversation any longer even though it seemed harmless. She did not answer and looked down at her hands. The man reacted immediately to her silence and said, "I am sorry. I did not mean to get personal"

Allie suddenly thought that she might have offended this well-meaning, talkative fellow traveler, so she put on a bright smile and said, "No, it is quite all right. I have had a long day, and I think I will make my way up to the restroom," and she rose in her seat.

With his best smile, the man said, "Of course, I understand. Can I call the flight attendant for you?"

"No, I'm fine," said Allie as she moved into the aisle and headed toward the front of the airplane.

"Mention my name and you'll get a good seat," said the man in a way to ease the sudden strain that was in the air by using the humor of a well-known joke.

Allie smiled as she moved up the aisle, glad that the short conversation with a stranger was at an end. The man unfolded his paper and once again buried his head, seemingly oblivious to his surroundings.

Once in the protective cocoon of the ladies' room, Allie looked in the mirror, thoughtfully contemplating the reflection of herself. "So, Allie," she said to herself, "just what are you doing? And more importantly, why are you doing it?" The face in the mirror soulfully looked back at her and did not smile. Allie persisted. "You could at least be decent enough to answer." Silence. Then she said, "Probably because there isn't an answer, at least not in the way you'd like." She splashed some cold water on her face, ran her fingers through her hair, and resisted the impulse to yawn.

Allie felt that if she thought about her situation, she might have a panic attack because everything that had happened to her in the last two days seemed as if it was out of a suspense novel. *How could this be?* she thought. Her hand went to the vial that hung around her neck, and it verified that it had definitely happened. She had given her word to that frightened little man back at Whispering Palms, Freedman Carver III. Allie remembered how terrified his eyes were. She had never seen anyone who looked that scared, and it was the reason she had agreed to help him.

She shook her head to erase the doubt that had crept in and realized that she had come this far on her word, and so she would continue this strange journey to its completion. It did not matter that she had given up her regular schedule and left work without telling anyone why or where she was going. She was committed to helping The Third, and she would see it through.

She took one last look into the mirror, and taking a deep breath, Allie prepared to leave the restroom and go back to her seat.

CHAPTER 11

Every Man for Himself

There was no noise in the room. It was as if there was no oxygen either as the men seated around the huge desk did not move. It seemed as if they were not breathing; they were so still. Finally, the man seated at the desk pulled a small black leather book from his inside jacket pocket, and he slowly flipped through the pages until he found what he was looking for. When he did speak, it was in a low monotone that did not reveal anything about his emotional state. Equally revealing was that the men listened and did not physically react.

"It's necessary," he said "that the goal be understood. The people we choose to use in this endeavor can never gain the complete knowledge of our goal. They must come away from any interaction with the positive feeling that they have penetrated our findings. This cannot be stressed enough. There is a line between the amount of understanding they have and the true picture of how they will react. It must continue to blend until it is unrecognizable."

There was a blanket of silence that descended upon the gathered men as they absorbed, digested, and agreed with the comments. One man spoke.

"So, when do we move out to initiate the plan?" The other men visibly relaxed as they nodded slightly to show they agreed. They would act when they received a sign from the dominant man.

The original speaker did not look up to give them any assurance, and he cleared his throat and continued to inspect the contours of the desk as if it held a secret he was silently contemplating.

Silence. And more silence. It was as if the air in the room was charged with an electricity that could almost be felt. Finally, he stood, and the other men jumped to their feet as if a sharp word had instructed them as one. He took some steps away from the group, and then he stopped. He turned and deliberately took a deep breath and fixed each man with a stare that they could not match as one by one, they lowered their gaze.

The man spoke into the air. "You will find the final instructions on your phones. Do not open them until I am no longer in your range of vision. Directions will be explicit to each person's history and training. This will be your last meeting at this location, and I expect each of you to meticulously follow instructions. While I prefer you apprehend the scientist alive, I do understand if that proves to be impossible. We must obtain one of the vials containing his serum so we can determine its molecular structure. The next time we meet, we must be in possession of the most crucial invention for mankind in this century. Whoever possesses the 'vial of life,' which he has so dramatically called it, will easily rule life as we know it on this earth." The man stopped talking and gazed at the exquisite wall covering as if it was the first time that he had seen it. He began to leave, but then he stopped and slowly turned to face the men.

"Gentlemen, I have ultimate faith that we are all on the same page in this venture. Possession of this vial and the serum it contains will make us not only rich beyond our dreams, but we will have global power unequaled in history." He abruptly turned on his heel, reminiscent of a military move, and before any of the men could react, he was gone.

The silence that followed almost yelled its presence as each man reached for his phone. There was no sharing of information as each man reverently protected the area around his phone. It was "every man for himself." While they may have to grudgingly work together, each man envisioned his future as the right-hand man in power beside their leader. Their egos did not allow them to realize that once he had the breakdown of the contents of the vial, they were immediately expendable. There would be no sharing of this wealth and power.

Once each man had digested the information on their phone, they all instantly realized they had another immediate problem. Who would move first? Suddenly, a low voice sliced through the air filling the room.

"Gentlemen, this is not a waiting room. You have your instructions. Leave now!"

They moved as one with downcast eyes, not risking the chance of eye contact. Somehow, they succeeded in making it through the single exit door without looking at or touching each other.

There was silence in the now empty room, and then a low rumble could be heard that built in its crescendo to a booming, guttural sound. The man who had given them the initial instructions on their phones was now enjoying a butt-gusting laugh that was tinged with a horrendously sinister echo. He reveled in the knowledge that one of these men would bring him the answers and the secret he demanded.

He knew he would not allow them to live after they delivered their findings, and his laughter indicated that he did not care. He would murder them without a second thought. It was this personal understanding of his greed and power that, for some strange reason, granted him this ability to laugh. He cared.

He cared greatly, but he cared only about himself and his need to rise to wealth and power.

CHAPTER 12

Fasten Your Seat Belt

Allie emerged from the restroom feeling more in control as she had made the decision to take this time on the plane to calmly go over all the events that had happened on this trip. In the past, Allie had found that when she was faced with a situation that appeared to be moving faster than she was comfortable with, it settled her mind if she mentally stepped back and rethought every move that brought her to that place in time. She had slept and eaten and the comfort level she felt within her own mind and body now gave her the strength to do this exercise.

Her steps fell lightly, and she felt a surge of renewed energy as she made her way down the aisle of the plane toward her seat. Suddenly, the plane jerked and rolled, sending her lurching across the aisle. Immediately, the "Fasten Your Seat Belt" sign came on, and the pilot's voice filled the cabin. He informed the passengers they were encountering some turbulence and to remain in their seats, keeping their seat belts fastened. The flight attendants dutifully moved through the cabin to make sure passengers complied. Allie had progressed down the aisle and was nearing her seat when another jerk of the plane sent her sprawling, and she literally fell into her seat.

The man with the newspaper and the apparent need to talk to her was immediately attentive and said, "Are you all right? That was quite a fall into your seat."

Allie was embarrassed he had witnessed her unladylike descent into her seat, and she laughed a little too loudly, insisting she was just fine. She busily searched for her seat belt as the attendant came to see if this passenger had survived her abrupt plunge into her seat, and would she like some water or coffee or tea?

In her mind, Allie wanted to say, "A stiff drink would be helpful, thank you," and she was immediately amazed that she would have thought of a stiff drink. It was so unlike her; however, she realized she was embarking on an adventure unlike any other she had experienced, and a stiff drink might be "just the ticket."

Allie settled into her seat and closed her eyes to clear her mind so she could think about the past twenty-four hours. Visions of her precious cat, Oreo, flashed in her mind's eye, and she felt a stabbing feeling of guilt, realizing he would be waiting for her to return. She was grateful that her neighbor, Mrs. Wilhelm, who had four cats of her own, would make sure that Oreo was fed and cared for in her absence. *Sorry, Oreo*, Allie thought. After this trip, she would be extra affectionate toward her feline roommate.

Suddenly, Allie felt as if she was not alone, and she opened her eyes to see the man who had spoken to her earlier was intensely watching her. She sat up in her seat, looked directly back at him, and said, "Excuse me. Is something wrong? Why are you staring at me?" Flustered, he broke his stare and immediately apologized.

"I am sorry. That was rude of me to stare, but your hair is the same color as my mother's, and I was admiring its richness and shine."

It was Allie's turn to be flustered and she nodded as she accepted his compliment. "Thank you. I inherited this head of hair from my mother's family," she said.

"Ah," he replied, "I do understand that 'from my side of the family' saying. I inherited my mother's height factor. She was six feet even, and my brothers and I all grew to be over six feet four inches in height."

"Oh my," said Allie. "Do you find the airplane seats uncomfortable because of your height?"

"No. The seats are just fine," he replied.

Allie mentally chided herself to stop any further conversation with this man because she needed the time to think. She settled back into her seat and closed her eyes, but her body decided that she needed sleep more than thinking, and within a few minutes, she fell asleep. The plane shuddered as it passed through unstable air, and the man glanced over at Allie, but she did not stir, so he felt certain she was already sound asleep.

The man, whose name was Blake Winters, relaxed back into his seat and opened a sleek leather case. He removed some papers and immediately began reviewing instructions he had received from the Department of Intelligence of the United States. He was reviewing the next steps in his assignment that informed him to follow Allie's movements.

His brow furrowed as he read, but his facial expression did not change. His training was to never reveal, by facial movements, any emotions that might alert a suspect as to what he was thinking or feeling. He periodically glanced across the aisle to see if Allie was still asleep. She slept soundly, not aware she was being watched. The instructions that Blake read were clear, concise, and to the point. He knew that he had to follow them to the letter if he was to be successful in his mission.

Blake and Allie were not aware that they were both being watched by a male passenger seated two rows away from them. He was associated with the Mexican cartel who were also interested in Freedman Carver III's serum. The cartel had not expected that Freedman Carver III would trust a female activities director at Whispering Palms with the vial of serum that they felt would change the future of the world. Time was suspended as the airplane droned its way north, carrying the extremely valuable cargo of Allie and the vial that nestled snugly around her neck.

For the moment, thousands of miles up in the sky, everyone was safe.

CHAPTER 13

Deep Breathing

The Third took a deep breath and exhaled slowly. He found that performing deep breathing exercises helped him when he was fighting stressful feelings. And he was having stressful feelings much more often these days. He thought back to when he did not need the deep breathing exercise. Back to a time when, though his many experiments invariably failed, it meant the battle with stress did not exist. Deep breath in. Hold the breath. Deep breath out.

He sighed. If only he had someone to talk to back then. If he had someone to share his anxieties toward stress, he was certain he would be able to control his body reactions. His phone vibrated in his pocket, and he reached in and fished it out to see it was his father. He was the last person he wanted to talk to.

The Third thought back to the days when his father lived in Texas and was only vaguely showing interest in his work. Last month The Third had reported a little progress with some growth of seeds to his father. The next thing he knew was that his father had made airplane reservations to fly in from Texas to be around to help him with the experiments.

The Third tried to tell his father that his arrival was far too early regarding his experiments, and while he was glad to see him, he should not plan on a long visit. His father, The Second literally harrumphed his reply to say that he would be the judge of when he should leave, if at all. He did not own property in Texas and was only renting an apartment, and he assured his son he had no time frame requiring his presence in Texas.

The Third felt the stressful feelings rise immediately, as the picture of his father being around to oversee his experiments was the last vision he wanted to imagine.

The Third began a prolonged series of inhaling and exhaling.

CHAPTER 14

A First Friendship

Allie was jolted awake as the plane shuddered and fought uneven pockets of air at thirty-two thousand feet. Her eyes darted around the dimness of the airplane, and then bit by bit her memory returned. She relaxed back into her seat and drew the airplane blanket around her, giving her the sense of being protected. *I miss Oreo*, she thought at the same time knowing that Mrs. Wilheim was caring for her precious feline roommate.

Slowly she let her mind become almost blank as she willed her memory banks to pull up the incidents of the past month. Allie could almost see her office, and she relished the protective feeling it always gave her. She brought the day to her mind when The Third had come to one of her activities. He looked so lost and out of place. She remembered going over to him to welcome him to the entertainment she had booked for the residents of Whispering Palms.

As she approached him, he looked as if he was ready to bolt from the room, so she put on her best I'm-here-to-help-you smile and spoke. "Mr. Carver, I am so happy you could join us this afternoon because the singing group that is here to entertain us are excellent. May I find you a seat up front?"

The Third opened his mouth to speak but succeeded only in looking like a fish gasping for air as no sound came out. He put his hands in his pockets and looked down at the floor and finally found the courage to say "Not up front."

Allie immediately understood as residents would often only sit in the back of the room because of their shyness, so she said, "Of course. There are a few seats in the back, and I like to sit there too, so why don't the two of us go and sit down and make ourselves comfortable?" She took his elbow and gently guided him toward the seats. When the entertainment was over, Allie turned to him and said, "I am so glad you could join us, and I hope you will be back again. We have entertainment here this time twice a week."

And The Third did come back the next week and the week after that as he found that Allie was the one human being who made him feel comfortable within himself. He found he liked that feeling very much.

And so it happened that over the coming weeks, The Third began to form a friendship with Allie.

CHAPTER 15

Where Can She Be?

Jim had stopped by the desk of his receptionist to ask that she contact Allie to ask her to come to his office for a meeting. "What do you mean she is not here? She is always here!" Jim did not mean to raise his voice. It just happened, and Gloria immediately replied, "Jim, for heaven's sake. You are yelling."

Jim started to reply he was not yelling, only to realize that he was indeed yelling, which surprised him because it was way out of his character to raise his voice. He stopped in his tracks and faced Gloria. "I am so sorry, Gloria. I will start again. I need to speak with Allie, but you are telling me she is not here. I know I didn't sign a vacation or a sick form for her, so I don't understand."

"Well, that makes two of us, Jim, because I did not sign anything either, and there are no telephone records of her signing out.

Speechless, they stared at each other in silence, and then Jim's demeanor changed. He looked at the floor and then back at Gloria. He spoke softly.

"Gloria, do you think something bad might have happened to her?" Her file says she lives alone, so maybe she is sick, or maybe she had a fall. "Will you pull up her file and find out who her emergency contact is and get me that information so I can make some calls."

"Of course. I will do that right away. Oh, Jim, do you really think something may be wrong?"

"I hope not. But it is a work day, and she is not here, and Allie is not the kind of employee who would suddenly not show up for work. It may be nothing more than her car broke down, but as our employee, we need to look out for her welfare. Please send the information to my office computer, and I will make the call."

Jim tried to sound as if it was a normal, matter-of-fact call, but as he turned and went to his office, both his heart and his stomach turned over with a dreadful feeling of what he would find.

CHAPTER 16

This Is Just So Perfect

The airplane droned on, and Allie kept her eyes closed as she willed herself to go over the events of the last month. She pictured Freedman Carver III's image of a little disheveled man who had come to live at Whispering Palms. *Bless his heart,* she thought as he reminded her of a lost soul who seemed to be constantly struggling to find himself but never quite achieving the process.

She thought back to the Friday evening when after working late and she was locking her office door, she turned to see him standing in the hallway. He was shifting from foot to foot and holding a large pot filled with soil. He looked so flustered that Allie immediately asked if she could help him. He put down the heavy pot, slowly looked up at her, and asked if she could help him with an ongoing experiment. Allie was used to the residents asking for help, so she said she would certainly be glad to help him if she could and waited for his explanation. It was not what she expected to hear.

Freedman Carver III cleared his throat and explained that he was doing an experiment with a serum of a fertilizer of sorts, and he wondered if Allie could keep the pot in her office where it was dark. He explained that he wanted to spread a liquid mixture in the soil and over some seeds while he left the pot in darkness.

Allie replied that she could certainly do that in her office; however, could he not do the same thing in a dark closet in his apartment? The Third did not hesitate as he shook his head "no" and said that he already had several pots occupying his apartment and was running out of room.

In her mind Allie had a flash of an apartment with huge pots of soil everywhere and wondered how the management would accept this way of living. However, it certainly was not a threat to anyone, and what harm could come of a form of indoor gardening?

Allie reached behind herself and deftly unlocked the door and snapped on the overhead lights. The Third meekly followed her into her office and deposited the pot in a dark corner. "This is just so perfect," he said. Then he noticed that Allie had a small night-light burning in the wall beside her desk. "We need to turn that light off," he said.

"Are you sure?" said Allie. It is just a little night-light."

The Third rubbed his eyes and pinched his forehead as if to brush away any residual pain and said, "For my experiment, I cannot have any light in the same area, and even a little night-light is too much."

"You're the boss," said Allie as she removed the light from its electrical socket. She looked around the office and noticed that light was filtering in from a window in the hallway. "Would you like me to pull down the blinds?" she said, and The Third almost sounded as if he would cry in gratitude.

"Oh yes, please," he said. "You have no idea how much this will do to help my experiment."

"Of course," said Allie, and she pulled down all the shades in her office, which resulted in a truly dark interior.

"Oh my. This is just so perfect," said The Third.

Allie said, "Well, it's Friday evening, and this room will be closed down like this until I come in on Monday."

By now The Third was almost ecstatic as he pulled a long cylindrical vial from his pocket, uncorked it, and proceeded to pour the contents into the soil. He repeated himself as he once again said, "This is perfect. Just so perfect." He looked at Allie and said, "When will you be here again?"

"On Monday morning about 8:45 AM," said Allie.

The Third was visibly excited as he repeated, "Perfect. That is just so perfect." Then he seemed to run out of adjectives, and he stood silent.

Allie was anxious to leave and get home to a cool glass of white wine with dinner with Oreo purring by her side, so she said, "Then, this is it, Mr. Carver?"

Her words broke his reverie with everything being so perfect, and he gave a little chuckle and said, "Of course. This is Friday night. Do you have big plans?" He rarely made conversation, but this question just seemed to bubble up out of him because he was truly grateful for Allie's help.

"No," she said. "The only Friday night plans I have involve having a little dinner and watching some television with my cat, Oreo. It has been a long day.

"Yes," he said. "I do notice that you give long hours to your job. You are very good at what you do."

This conversation seemed to come easily from him when in truth, he was usually so uncomfortable around other humans that he rarely talked to the other residents, but somehow Allie's presence relaxed him. It was as if she exuded a spirit of kindness and acceptance, which immediately affected those around her to relax, and it was affecting The Third. He spoke again.

"My experiment is toward the encouragement of growth," he said. "I hope that the ingredients of the serum in the vial will stimulate the seeds that I have introduced to the serum, and once it meets with the soil, normal growth will be instantly exaggerated and even be better in quality and quantity than if the seeds had been generously watered and exposed to copious amounts of sunlight."

It was the most Allie had ever heard this little man say, and she was not quite sure what an appropriate response would be. When she did not speak, he continued his explanations.

"In my scientific findings, I am trying to develop a serum that will be able to generate growth even in the absence of water and sunlight, so this room is," he looked around and then appeared to be talking to himself, "this room is perfect. It is just so perfect."

Then he fell silent again, and Allie cleared her throat and jiggling her keys and said enthusiastically for his benefit, "Then I'm so glad it's so perfect, and I guess we'll meet back here on Monday morning."

Allie suddenly realized she was hungry and tired and anxious to get home to snuggle with her feline roommate. Oreo would purr as soon as she came in the door. She would sit and stroke him, letting the purring sound surround her consciousness, and she could literally feel the stresses of the day fall away. She thought that the sound of a cat contentedly purring was the most precious sound. It seemed to envelope her, infusing a kind of grateful presence to be in the company of her pet that seemed more like a person to her than an animal.

The Third was again exhibiting a kind of withdrawal from his outburst of speaking, and so together they turned off the overhead lights and walked out into the hallway. She locked the door to her office as The Third was again muttering to himself, "Oh, this is perfect. It is just so perfect."

"All righty then," Allie brightly said. "We will meet back here on Monday morning at 8:30 AM, and we can check on your…your…" She did not know what to call it and finally said, "Your experiment."

"Oh yes," he said. "This is going to be so good. "I'll see you Monday morning." He managed a little smile, and Allie immediately smiled back.

"Monday morning it is. Would you like me to walk you back to your apartment? It is on my way out."

This bit of kindness seemed to stun The Third, and he said, "Why, that would be very kind of you. I do not often get escorted by a lovely young woman like you. I consider it a delightful offer. Thank you."

Once again, he seemed stymied by the number of words he had spoken and fell awkwardly silent again. Allie led the way down the hall, and soon they were standing in front of his apartment door. Neither seem to know what to say in parting, and The Third rose to the occasion as he once again thanked her for helping him with his experiment adding, "it is just so perfect."

Allie was gracious in her enthusiasm and said, "I hope we find your serum will have created a happy and healthy crop of...of something," she said.

Grass," he said. "I used grass seed."

"Okay then," said Allie. "Hopefully we'll see some sprigs of green on Monday morning."

"Yes, hopefully," he mirrored her wording. "Thanks again for your help," and he turned the key in his door.

Allie walked on down the hall to give him the privacy of entering his home. "See you Monday morning," she said.

"Yes. Monday morning," he said, and stepping inside his apartment, he quietly closed the door.

CHAPTER 17

The Happening

Allie moved down the hallway thinking about how this meeting had been so interesting. She was inwardly grateful she had been in the right place tonight to assist this meek little man with his science experiment. With that thought, she put the meeting out of her mind and hurried her step a little as she was already anxious to be home with her purring roommate at her side.

Allie had established the beginning of her friendship with The Third. It was indeed a matter of being in the right place at the right time that he needed help with somewhere to put his pot of soil. Neither would have imagined that their new friendship would prosper and grow into a wonderfully solid "happening."

Allie fondly remembered that her grandmother, who was a delightfully social woman, would call the friendships she made with others "happenings." She told Allie that she always considered friendships to be the wonderful happenings that graced her life. Everywhere she went she formed various happenings, and she even had a way of making each new meeting an occasion.

Her happenings each had a scale of her own invention, and she mentally labeled them. "This happening was a three because I met them only briefly," the grandmother would announce to her granddaughter. Other happenings had higher values on her scale determined by how long the meeting was or by the length of time they knew each other.

Allie found it quite confusing, but it brought her grandmother so much happiness that Allie went along with it. And so it was that Allie began a happening with the scientist known as The Third. And neither member of this new happening could foresee how it would affect both of their lives.

Allie always wondered why, for people who were working and their off times were the weekends, it seemed that the weekend days seemed to fly by far quicker than the weekdays. And so it was that she felt she had just awakened to a Saturday morning when it was suddenly Sunday evening, and she was preparing for the workweek to begin again.

She was making her way to her office to begin the week when she suddenly remembered the pot of dirt that she had placed there with Mr. Freedman Carver the Friday before. She had not once thought about it over the weekend, but now she realized she was anxious to see if anything had happened. It was just 8:30 AM, and as she approached her office, she saw that Mr. Carver III was there waiting for her to arrive.

"Good morning," Allie said cheerfully, and Mr. Carver III seemed genuinely pleased to see her.

"Good morning," he said. "I hope you had a wonderful weekend."

"Yes, I did," Allie replied, "but it always seems to go by so very quickly, and the next thing I know, it's Monday again, and I am back at work. I am sorry, but I must admit I did not give your pot of dirt much thought."

The Third chuckled and said that was to be expected.

"However, I am anxious to see if there might be any growth of the grass seeds," Allie said, "so let me unlock my office door, and we can go in together and see what we shall see."

Allie turned the key in the lock and was rewarded with a loud swooshing sound as the door swung open. Affecting a "here-we-come" voice, she said aloud to the office, "Okay, grass seed. Here we come to check on you." Allie flicked the overhead light on, and together they entered the office.

What they saw stopped them both in their tracks. The lone pot of dirt had produced a most prolific growth of grass, which stood about twelve inches in height. There was so much weight that the grass not only reached up toward the ceiling, but it arched over the rim of the pot and reached to the floor. Allie was stunned and stood perfectly still unable to speak.

The Third was also speechless for a few seconds, but then he said, "Oh my goodness. It is so much more than I expected. It is just so perfect."

Allie looked at The Third and said, "What exactly did you expect? You planted some grass seeds without water, fertilizer, or light, and now you have," lost for descriptive words, she said, "Mr. Carver, I believe you have a farm."

"Yes," he said, grinning like the Cheshire Cat. "It seems I do have a farm on my hands."

Allie said, "So what do you do now?"

Ever the scientist, he said, "So now I will take this back to my room and do some tests to determine if it is the same grass seed that I planted last Friday. From there, I will write a scientific paper to cover this experiment and to also ensure that I document the results correctly." He turned to Allie. "I would be grateful if I could enlist you as an assistant with this experiment. You were with me when we left this pot of dirt last Friday afternoon, and you are with me again when we see it on this Monday morning."

Allie was amazed at his request, and she hesitated to reply, and The Third took it that her silence meant that she was not willing to be associated with his experiment. "I understand," he said. "You are very busy, and I won't ask you to help with the findings."

Allie finally found her voice and said, "Oh no. It is just the opposite. I would be delighted to help you document this growth," she said with an admiring, wonder-struck voice. The two stood silently looking at the "farm," and neither spoke. Finally, Allie realized that they should be doing something with this farm, and she asked if she could help him take it back to his room.

"No, thank you," said The Third. "I have a little dolly in my room that I use to move heavy pots of soil around my apartment. I will go and bring the dolly so I can move it from your office. And," he said, "please know how grateful I am to have another human witness this growth from my experiment."

Allie was still dumbstruck over the huge growth of grass, but she also felt that it might have been a fluke, and the only way to proceed would be to do the same experiment with other plants. As The Third went to get his dolly to move the pot, she had to inwardly smile as this "farm" might prove to be an interesting event. She was glad to have been at "the right place at the right time" and included in his experiment. Showing the ability to really hustle, The Third appeared with a small dolly, and together they succeeded in moving the pot with its overflowing growth of grass onto the dolly.

"Please know how much I appreciate this," he said and, in almost the same breath, added, "I would like to take you up on your generous offer to give me some more help with my experiments."

Without waiting for her to answer, he plunged ahead with his words tumbling out over each other. "I have a vial containing the liquid I used for this experiment, and I would be most grateful if you would consider keeping this for me. I put it on a chain so that you can wear it around your neck for safekeeping."

Allie was stunned at his prolific outpouring of words and then to realize that he wanted her to wear the vial around her neck. She answered immediately in her enthusiasm. "No, I mean yes, I will be more than glad to help you with your experiment. But," she said more slowly, "are you sure I need to wear this around my neck?"

His answer was loud and immediate. "Oh, most definitely around your neck. I need for it to be in a safe place, and if you wear it around your neck, I know it will be safe."

Again, he surprised himself with his dialogue, and he plunged his hands into his pockets and lowered his head to inspect the floor. Then, more slowly, he said, "Perhaps I've overstepped my bounds as I didn't mean to…"

Allie interrupted him. "No, Mr. Carver, around my neck will be just fine. I am more than happy to help you."

His demeanor immediately changed, and he almost appeared to be lighter and younger in his appearance. "Thank you," he said.

Slowly he held out the vial that was on the necklace, and Allie smoothly slipped it over her head. Then The Third immediately picked up the dolly's handles and carefully maneuvered the pot with its overflow of growth down the hallway and back to his apartment.

Allie watched his back as he went down the hall and could only shake her head. *I can't wait to tell all this to Oreo*, she thought. It was something Allie had always done. Each night after work, she would speak aloud to her feline roommate, telling her of the events that filled her days at work.

This, thought Allie, would prove to be a very long story and interesting story to share with Oreo.

CHAPTER 18

A Piece of Jewelry

"What do you mean you do not have the vial of life?" boomed the voice from the phone. "I gave you explicit orders to obtain the vial contents so I can get a lab to analyze it so we can replicate the contents. If this 'liquid' can increase plant growth beyond all our present abilities, it will be literally worth its weight in gold, and now it seems you are telling me you cannot break into his apartment and get that vial? You had best not let me think that I have hired the wrong men for this job."

The three men who were gathered around the cell phone looked "wilted" as they had to tell "the voice" that they were not able to find the vial in The Third's room. One of them spoke.

"We had to wait until he left the room, and he only left it for an hour when he went to hear some people singing."

"And," said another man, "he has stopped going down to the dining room for meals and has them sent up to his room, so he rarely leaves."

"Even so," the voice boomed. "How hard could it have been to search the room once and find the vial?"

A third man spoke. "When we couldn't find it, we increased our observation of him, and he took the vial with him to the activities directors' office, and when he returned, he did not have it."

There was a long pause and then the voice said, "So you are telling me that the activities director has the vial? Why would he give it to her? She has not been taking part in his experiments." He paused. In a measured voice he said, "So, you are saying that he gave her the vial, and when she leaves it in her office, it should not be hard to break in and get it, so what are you waiting for? And if you think I am getting fed up with waiting for you to complete this assignment, you would be correct."

One man spoke. "Of course, we have done our observations and would certainly do that if she left the vial in her office. However, it seems she is wearing it on a chain around her neck."

"And just why would she do that?" boomed the voice."

The spokesman continued. "Apparently because he asked her to. He put the vial on a chain, and she wears it all day, and it even goes home with her. It is like a piece of jewelry."

Another man took over the conversation. "So, it seems the scientist is very aware of the value of the vial and does not trust the security of his apartment. It is obvious he is hiding in plain sight as he chooses to live in an old folks' home. It's a brilliant move because no one would think to look there."

There was a long painful pause until the voice spoke again. "Gentlemen, I am leaving it up to you to get me that vial. I do not want to know how you plan to do it, but neither do I want any adverse publicity connected with this, so I would suggest you not use violent measures. I will plan to give you time to achieve your assignments. Advise me when you have the vial in your possession."

As quietly as he had joined their conversation, he signed off. The three men did not move, and it was as if they were frozen statues. Then, as if on a silent cue, all three moved as one, and each man, with cell phone in hand, spoke in hushed tones as they connected with other men and delivered the news, asking for more assistance with their assignment.

And with this conversation, The Third and Allie would find themselves under the constant surveillance of the Mexican cartel.

CHAPTER 19

Communication Problems

Allie was at her desk in her office and was so engrossed in her work she did not hear that someone had knocked very softly at her open office door. The Third was standing in her office doorway, watching Allie work, and he wished that he was many years younger. He would have wanted to ask this lovely woman out to have dinner with him. Then he smiled to himself because he realized that as a young man, he was much too shy, and so he had buried himself in his scientific studies and experiments. The chance to ask anyone out never happened. He suddenly felt as if he was out of place and invading her privacy watching her work, so he knocked on the door again.

Allie looked up and seeing The Third, she smiled and rose to greet him. Her sudden smile startled him, and he took a step back and then immediately looked down at the floor.

"Hello, Mr. Carver. How nice to see you out and about. Is there anything I can do to help you today?" When he did not answer and seemed to be flustered and tongue-tied, Allie spoke again. "As you can see, I am wearing the vial around my neck," and she held it up for him to see.

"Oh yes. Thank you very much for doing that. I came to see if I could speak with you privately as I have run into something of a problem, and I might need your help with…things." After his outburst of words, he shifted from foot to foot and looked down at the floor.

"Of course," said Allie. "Please come into my office, and we can close the door so we'll have privacy." Allie rose from her desk and indicated that he could sit in a chair at her desk. She moved to close the office door. She walked back to her desk and sat down in her chair and said, "There we go. I can assure you we have complete privacy."

"Thank you," he said, but then he suddenly seemed at a loss for words, so Allie spoke to bridge the silence. "How is your farm doing? If it grows anymore, we may have to get you a larger apartment." She chuckled at her joke as she realized he seemed to be very serious, and she wanted to lighten things up for him.

"Well," he said matching her nickname of the growth, "my farm has continued to grow, and I have had to cut it back several times. He did not smile but forced himself to continue. I have been very busy duplicating the formula, but I do not have the room to make much serum, and I have run into a problem in sending it to my lab for safekeeping.

Allie did not speak, giving him the space to talk. He took a deep breath and continued with his explanation.

"I have run into some…ah…communication problems, and it is most unusual." He cleared his throat and pressed on with his speech. "I have a personal laboratory that I established many years ago, and I send my experiments there for documentation and safekeeping. The lab is run by a good friend of mine that I went to college with. His name is Lenny. However, when I have tried to contact him, I do not get an answer, and that is most unusual. He lives alone, and now I am worried. He does not answer his phone and has not returned any of my emails. It has been several days now, and I was wondering if it might be my connections on this end and so I…"

The Third had been speaking nonstop and seemed to be out of breath with the effort, and so Allie spoke to help him.

"Oh my goodness, I understand, and you must be very worried about your friend. Do you know anyone in his family that you can contact?"

Thankful for her help, The Third regained his ability to speak and said, "My friend was an only child, and both parents are deceased. I do not know of any other family members."

Anxious to help this shy little man who apparently needed help with some ideas, Allie said, "Well, I can see that you are very worried." Allie paused as she considered her next words. "As you know the town where he lives, perhaps you could contact the local police and explain that you are concerned that you cannot reach your friend and ask if they might go to his address and check on him for you?"

The Third wished he had thought of that idea and not have to bother this young lady, and so he said, "Oh, thank you. I wish I had thought to do that." The Third had a habit of making a statement and then pausing, as if he still had more to say, but then not immediately speaking. This gave the other person in the conversation the strange feeling of wondering if he had finished and if it was their turn to talk. Allie had become used to this quirk in his manner of speech, so she immediately spoke.

"If you would like, I can call the police department from my office, and you could speak to them and ask if they would check on your friend."

The Third would have loved to have Allie do that for him, but instead, he said, "Thank you, but no. I have taken up more of your time than is necessary, and I will call again from my apartment. Thank you again for giving a solution to this old man," and he rose and, without further dialogue, he turned and left her office.

Allie sat in silence as she looked at the space opposite her desk that moments ago was filled by The Third. She was used to the elderly residents being set in their ways and adverse to any change or offers of help, but she wished he had agreed to let her call for him.

She shook her head to brush away her thoughts and turned her attention to the document she was working on.

CHAPTER 20

Three Blind Mice

The three Mexican men given the assignment of finding the vial had each devised a different plan and approach to their problem. The first man decided to park his car outside the building housing the city lab, and then he would follow whoever had the job of delivering the vial to its owner.

The second man went to the city to search the public records to see if the vial had been registered to anyone other than The Third.

The last man felt his best bet would be to shadow the man who worked at the lab and follow him and frighten him into giving him information about the contents of the vial. He would then arrange to have the serum duplicated and receive his reward from his handler, "The Voice." He could almost taste the delight of punishing his next victim, and he could hardly wait to begin. His head would throb with expectation, not unlike that of a migraine headache; however, he did not know that his delight bordered on that of a mentally sick, psychotic mind.

The three men knew that the one constant they all had was the knowledge that the man known as Freedman Carver III held the secret they all wanted to solve. It was only a matter of time before one of them would succeed, and each man was certain that he would be the successful one.

It would seem that The Third would have no opportunity to evade the intense scrutiny of these three men. They all felt that he was, in effect, toast, and each man felt that there was no way that the little elderly scientist had a chance against their youth.

Of course, The Third was vaguely aware that he might be in danger. His thoughts went to the one situation he had created entirely on his own and that only one other person knew of its existence—Lenny.

The Third had decided early on in his scientific, experimental upbringing that he was alone, and being so alone was a dangerous situation. He did not trust his father. He did not think him to be a bad person, but he knew his father was uneducated in understanding the world of science. His father did not comprehend that the possibility of untold riches often led men to do foolish and vicious things. And so outwardly, The Third had gone along with his father's bidding.

On his own, he had researched the Internet until he was secure in his knowledge of it, and then, he asked one of his classmates from college, Lenny, to create a laboratory in his basement. Lenny lived alone in a little town just below the Arctic Circle called Kensington. Lenny and The Third had shielded each other from the oppressive bullying that enveloped them in high school for being the class geeks in science and math. It would make them lifelong friends.

The lab was funded by The Third, and it was to serve as the safe place in case any of his experiments worked. That is why the vial containing the latest ingredients that produced "the farm" would be sent to Lenny to be placed in this secret laboratory. This lab would prove to be the ultimate secret place that would allow The Third to advance his knowledge far beyond that of a single unknown scientist.

In the world of scientific achievements, it might even rise to that of a rock star.

CHAPTER 21

A Nice Guy Smile

The Third felt the weight of the oppressive stress as his mind began to realize the enormity of the success of what he and Allie jokingly referred to as the farm. He fell back onto the sofa and lost himself in his world of inhaling and exhaling until that action wrapped him in a cocoon-like blanket. He allowed himself to remain within this protected state. For the moment, The Third was at peace because he was unaware of the three men who had rented an apartment at Whispering Palms so they could watch his every move.

The Third sat perfectly still and thought about his options. He could continue to use his phone or his computer to try to reach his friend Lenny, or he could do as Allie had suggested and contact the police. If Lenny was indeed in trouble because of illness or a fall, contacting the police would be a good thing to do. However, if Lenny had just decided to go on a weekend trip, alerting the police would let them know of the secret laboratory, and The Third did not want that.

He was quite certain that Lenny would have told him if he had planned to be away, and that knowledge gave The Third the almost certain knowledge that something was terribly wrong. He decided to wait a few more hours and try to contact him one more time, and if he did not answer, only then would he alert the police to his dilemma.

The Third suddenly realized how tired he was, and so he sat back on his comfy sofa and closed his eyes. When he was better rested, he would try to reach Lenny again. The sofa seemed to completely understand his need to rest, and it offered its warmth and softness. Within minutes The Third was softly snoring and oblivious to the passage of time.

A week had passed since Allie had spoken to The Third, and as she stood at the back of the room during the weekly entertainment, she decided she would drop by his apartment to check on him once all the residents had gone to dinner.

As Allie stood outside his apartment door, she hesitated and did not knock. As was her usual custom, she replayed her thoughts that brought her to the door of The Third. *Perhaps I should just leave it be*, she thought to herself. *If Mr. Carver needed my help, he would have come to my office. But what if something has happened to him?* Suddenly, his apartment door opened, and he stepped out into the hall, forcing Allie to take a step backward. Each was equally startled, and they stood looking at each other, making solid eye contact.

Allie was immediately startled to see the change in The Third. His appearance was of someone who was lacking in sleep with deep bags beneath his eyes. He had not shaved, and his hair resembled a mop of unkempt curls badly in need of a comb. His clothing was wrinkled beyond repair. Allie was speechless and could do nothing but stare, and so The Third was the first to regain his composure and speak.

"Ah, Miss Allie. I was just coming down to your office. I really need," he stammered," I really need to speak with you. Let me get my briefcase, and we can go to your office."

Allie finally found her voice. "Why don't we just talk in your apartment?" she offered.

The Third immediately replied, "Oh no. We cannot do that. Your office is much safer." And he disappeared back into his apartment.

Allie's mind was racing. *What does he mean, my office is safer? Safer from what?* And then her thoughts changed direction. *He looks so terrible*, she thought. *"Maybe he has had a small stroke and is not thinking clearly."* She made a mental note to contact the Nurses Unit to see if she could get him checked out.

The Third came bustling out of his apartment so fast that Allie had to step backward. He had his briefcase in one hand and; with the other, he grabbed her elbow and literally moved for them both as he pushed her down the hallway toward her office.

Still speechless, Allie went with him, and when they reached her office, he went in first and reached back to guide her in. He immediately shut the door. He faced her and said, "Please sit down. We need to talk."

Allie obediently sat in one of the two chairs by her desk, and The Third put his briefcase on the desk and faced her. He took a huge breath as if to inhale most of the oxygen, and then he stopped and gazed at the floor.

In the sudden onset of silence, Allie regained her composure and started to speak. "Mr. Carver, I hope that…"

Suddenly, The Third stood up straight, held up his hand, and interrupted her. "Please," he said forcefully, then speaking quieter, he said, "Please. Let me explain." Allie relaxed and sat back in the chair, and The Third recognized her motion as giving him permission to continue speaking.

The Third took a deep breath and began. "Miss Allie, it is about my experiment that we called the farm. I need your immediate help." He went on to tell her about his missing friend, Lenny, who lived near the Arctic Circle and about his father trying to oversee his work and how he sensed that men with criminal backgrounds were stalking him. He even included facts about his friend David who had helped him in the past.

When he finished, Allie sat ever so still and was almost afraid to speak as her mind was whirling. She tried, in vain, to imagine that he was having a mental breakdown; however, when she looked in his eyes, she could see a man who was totally in control of himself and who was desperately asking for her help.

Allie made an immediate decision and took a deep breath and said, "So what would you like me to do?"

CHAPTER 22

A Matter of Time

The Third opened the door to his apartment and immediately crumpled into a heap on the sofa. "Good lord," he said out loud, as if the sound of his voice would give him the support that he so desperately craved. Then he began to laugh, slowly at first, but then the laughter bubbled out of him, filling his small apartment. He laughed until he could no longer breathe, and once silent, he fell back onto the sofa and fixed his gaze on the ceiling.

He spoke to the silence of the apartment, needing to feel as if he were not alone. "I did it. Oh my god, I did it." He suddenly sat upright, his eyes fixed on the farm. "It's so much more." He searched for the best adjective, and finding none, he moved into his mind and talked from there. It was an exercise he had developed as a young man when he was alone in his basement laboratory. It was as if he was speaking out loud, but within the silence of his prolific scientific thoughts.

He had just come from Allie's office, and he spoke to himself. "I'm sure I did the right thing when I trusted Allie with that vial, and now that I know the correct specifications of the serum, I am quite certain." He was still for a moment as he replayed his thoughts in his mind. "No, I am very certain it is only a matter to time that the men who might want to steal this serum for their use will be trying to find me. It is best that she has the vial."

Back in his office at Whispering Palms, Jim was finding out that Allie's emergency contact had not spoken to her in months and did not know there was any trouble. Gloria, the receptionist, was also striking out as she called a few of the friends they shared only to realize that no one was aware that Allie was even missing.

At Whispering Palms there was a growing feeling that something was very, very wrong as one by one, the residents began asking about Allie's absence in their lives. No one thought to ask any of the residents if they knew where Allie might have gone. And so, no one asked The Third.

He was the only person who knew the reason for Allie's sudden disappearance and where she was and why.

CHAPTER 23

A Missed Approach

It was the time of the year when the air was crisp and the trees were erupting into marvelous hues of orange, yellow, and red. People took special trips to states where these trees grew, intent on nothing else but drinking in the colors of the fall season.

No such colorful seasonal transformation happens in Florida. Palm trees reach to the sky with stovepipe-looking trunks with no branches, and awkward, ugly bursts of prickly, twisted growths sprout from their tops. St. Augustine grass creeps and covers the ground in a dull and uninspiring brownish-green hue, while the only flowers that bloom are hidden in dense hedges. The sun beats down daily with punishing heat, allowing only the hardiest plants to survive.

The humidity is crippling and each day, around 3:00 PM, clouds in the sky open, and angry, pelting rain beats down. The raindrops are so dense that if one is caught in the deluge, they are immediately soaked to their skin. On the freeways, cars pull over and wait because windshield wipers cannot function as the rain beats down. Suddenly, the rain stops as quickly as it began, and the sun regains its dominance, causing the air to feel like that of a sauna bath.

Locals willingly stay inside homes or stores; however, tourists who are tanning on the beaches or shopping or biking are constantly surprised by the monsoon attack from the skies. It is a shared delight that locals observe and silently laugh at the stunned tourists who are inevitably doused by Mother Nature's afternoon Florida rainstorms.

And so it was that the three Mexican cartel members, who were posing as tourists, found themselves "trapped" on an afternoon at 3:00 PM. Mexico's weather does not have monsoon-type rainstorms.

The first Mexican made the mistake of leaving his car to run to a nearby building, and he ended up huddling against the outside of the "locked" building, cold to the bone and shocked at the violence of the storm. He had not been happy with the assignment he had been given, and this episode pushed him over the edge as he made plans to return to Mexico on the next flight out.

The second Mexican was crossing a street as he came from purchasing some cigarettes at a dollar store, and he sprinted to his car to collapse in the front seat as the rainstorm followed him inside. He was forced to sit out the storm in his car as he shivered uncontrollably. Overnight his asthma would erupt, landing him in a private clinic and pulling him out of the hunt for the elusive vial.

The last Mexican cartel member was the unluckiest of the three men with his initial introduction to Florida weather. He was in the middle of a large park that had only a few scraggly palm trees offering nothing in the way of shelter. Far across the open park were some benches that surrounded a lone porta-potty, and he ran for the protection of the small building. Once inside, greeted by the overwhelming odor because it had not been serviced in many months, he almost fainted and bolted back outside into the deluge of rain. After throwing up, he stood surveying the area. There was nowhere to go, and so he dejectedly moved to the lone bench.

His rain-filled shoes squeaked with every step as huge rivers of water cascaded down his forehead as he endured the rainstorm, silently cursing his profession. He was a most pitiful sight, and at that moment, he did not look like a dangerous and proud, card-carrying member of the Mexican cartel. He very much resembled a drowned little rat.

And so it was that the uncomfortable, wet condition acted as fuel for his determination, and he retreated into his mind to review the instructions he had received about the vial.

It made him the most dangerous threat that Allie would face in her race to the Arctic Circle.

CHAPTER 24

Where Was She?

The voice of the pilot came over the sound of the engines as he advised the passengers that they were approaching the Seattle airport. The airplane cabin lights came on to illuminate the disheveled passengers who were struggling to adjust to the sudden change from their cocoon-like hibernation of the long flight.

The man sitting opposite Allie spoke. "Thank you for listening to my troubles about my niece," he said. "Not everyone would have been so understanding."

Allie felt bad she had tried to ignore him after their initial conversation, and she answered him with her usual open friendliness. "No problem. I do understand how hard it is to see one of your family go through a difficult time," she said, not realizing she was giving him the opening that he wanted to continue their dialogue.

"No," he said. "I am grateful for your kindness, and I would like to do something to thank you. Perhaps we could have a cup of coffee when we land at the airport. Or maybe even have lunch if you have the time." He gave her his best "I am really a nice guy" smile.

Allie hesitated, and that was all he needed. "I tell you what," he said. "When we land, I will pick up our luggage and meet you at the terminal restaurant. It's right in the middle of the airport. Has a decent menu considering it serves airport food, and that will save you having to fight the crowds getting their luggage."

He continued, not giving Allie the chance to speak. "Honestly, it's the least I can do, and I would really love to have a meal before I have to fight the traffic." He looked directly into her eyes and said," Please let me do this. Airports and traveling can be such a pain, and a good meal would make us both feel better."

Allie suddenly felt thankful that someone else was making the decisions, and so she handed him her luggage tags and said, "This is really nice of you…"

"Blake," he said. "Blake Winters and your name is?"

"Allie," she said. "Allie Birks. Nice to meet you, Blake."

Allie settled back into her seat and relaxed as the plane began its descent through the frigid air as it gently floated down toward the sphere of the earth. The motion gave the weary passengers the feeling that they were in a safe cocoon-like bubble ever so gently gliding toward a smooth reintroduction to the gravity of earth.

The passengers of flight 1911 did not realize the pilots were silently fighting to hold the giant fuselage from whipping from side to side in the stiff winds that were blowing across the runway. The captain was a grizzled man who was nearing the end of his career. His knuckles were white with the exertion of the deathlike grip that he used to control the whipping of the huge plane as it fought the landing.

His copilot was a young, baby-faced man in his early forties who was making his first flight to the Arctic region. He could not speak or move because of the fear that he was experiencing as the huge plane dropped closer to the runway. Only the noise of the screaming engines filled the cockpit as the captain used all his strength and experience to control the landing. He instinctively knew that his petrified copilot would not be of any help, and just as he made the final approach to kiss the runway with the descending wheels, he threw his weight back into the seat. With all his strength he pulled back on the stick as he executed what the airplane industry calls a "missed approach to the runway." The giant airplane shuddered with the execution of the change of direction, and finally it slowly obeyed the captain's demand to rise above the runway and lift its nose back toward the ice-blue sky.

The passengers were suddenly roughly and unceremoniously thrown forward, and then their bodies were pressed back into their seats. They were at the mercy of the harsh movement of a giant fuselage that was being subjected to the whiplash motion of almost landing to suddenly and angrily being hurled back into the sky.

Allie was brutally whipped from being a passenger who was totally relaxed with her eyes closed to harshly experiencing the sudden, painful explosion of being pressed back into her seat. She found it difficult to breathe, move, or speak as the plane inched slowly upward, and then finally gaining the speed needed to punch its way back up through the dense atmosphere, it stopped shuddering and leveled out.

The screaming sound of engines changed to a soft purring sound as they were no longer forced to pull against the atmosphere. Each passenger found themselves overwhelmed with the sudden knowledge they had somehow survived a horrible ending to their flight. They each gave silent thanks to their God of choice first and the airplane crew second.

The airline attendants were able to find their voices as they filled the airplane with their words, informing the passengers that all was well and that the pilots had the situation in control. They droned on as they explained that a "missed approach to the runway" did not mean that they missed the approach to the runway. In pilot-speak it meant that there had been a sudden wind that crossed the runway as the plane was making its final approach to landing, causing the pilot to make the decision to go around to make another attempt at landing. It was all very normal they said. They fooled no one in the cabin. Everyone was quiet as they grappled with their intimate thoughts of how they all had just survived a close call.

From two seats back in the plane, the man who was following both Allie and the man across from her spoke quietly into his cell phone. He was telling his contact they would soon land in Seattle and he needed new instructions to complete his assignment. Only when he hung up did he allow himself to admit that he had been frozen with fear as the gyrations of the plane twisted in the frozen air. He was not a man of faith, but he found himself searching to acknowledge a higher power within his mind and to give thanks for the grace of being saved.

There was a silence in the cabin as the plane dipped within a few feet of touching down, and Allie realized she had been holding her breath. Her chest felt as if an army was walking across it, and she could not move. Her mind knew she must breathe, but her paralyzed body was in charge. Ever so slowly she sat a little taller and slowly willed her lungs to expand. When she found she could feel the sensation of breath within her body, she gratefully allowed herself to begin to accept the oxygen that fed her being with a strength of knowing she was once again in control. One breath gave way to another, and she found herself thinking of how The Third would have weathered this near-death experience.

The sound of the wheels screaming against the runway brought her mind into focus, and a smile crossed her face as she told herself it was all for the best that she was there and he was not.

CHAPTER 25

Missing in Action

Back at Whispering Palms, it seemed that everyone knew that something was very wrong because Allie was not at work. The residents missed her even though some enterprising soul had decided that she must be on vacation and had passed the word as if they knew it to be a truth. However, Allie's employer knew that she was not on vacation, and Jim had been wrestling with the thought that something must be very wrong. Allie seemed to have vanished into thin air without a trace, and no one seemed to know what had happened.

Jim was torn with the knowledge that she was a valued employee who had not applied for vacation or requested a leave of absence. She was not one who would not show up for work. He knew she lived alone. Her emergency contact had not been advised of any absence. She did not list any family members in her file. She lived with a cat. What should he do?

Informing the police seemed like a huge invasion of her privacy, but Jim told himself he was concerned about her well-being and safety and not prying into her life outside of her work. What should he do? He decided to have his secretary contact the nearby local hospitals in case she had the need to go to an emergency room. She might have slipped and fallen and twisted an ankle, or perhaps she had a virus and needed help in quieting an aggressive stomach. Jim suddenly realized that his head hurt terribly with the kind of headache that screams of tension threatening to obliterate one's sense of logical thinking. Jim wished that this problem in managing his new position had not raised its head to confuse and overtake his day. What had happened? Where could she be? What more could he do? He decided to go through her personnel file one more time to see if he had missed anything. His headache now throbbed with every sudden move of his head as he opened Allie's file.

The words in front of him were almost a blur that seemed to shout that he would find nothing new.

CHAPTER 26

Within His Breath

If The Third had been more of a resident who was in the loop for gossip, he would have heard that people were talking and wondering why Allie had not been at work. Allie's sunshiny presence was like a medicinal balm to most of the residents as they all looked forward to her presence when her all-encompassing smile told them all was well at Whispering Palms.

The residents who were able to keep up with comings and goings had decided that Allie must be on vacation. If she was sick, the front desk would have put out a notice and someone would have been brought in to take her place. Someone like Allie would not just disappear, and so the rumors began to bubble up through their limited network of gossip.

One romantic resident who always thought that Allie was a wonderful woman who should be married to a wonderful man suggested that she might have eloped. Once she had enjoyed a marvelous honeymoon, she would once again return to be the bright light in their lives. This suggestion did not last long as the more pragmatic pointed out that Allie was the kind who would deserve the joy of a huge wedding complete with all the trimmings, and so she would not have eloped.

However, the rumors only lasted as long as their minds could wrap around their thoughts. Their advanced ages and their need for afternoon naps meant that none would dwell too long on imaginary stories about her absence. They decided that Allie would soon return, and so they napped and played cards and bingo and ever so patiently waited for Allie's return.

Someone knew where Allie was, and The Third was not sharing his knowledge. He did not even realize that her absence was a subject of controversy. His world was like a small enclosed vessel. He could not begin to envision that her absence was a topic that not only the residents but the staff were discussing. The Third could only function in the present, and his present was filled with the knowledge of only two things. One was that his friend Lenny was suddenly missing in action. And the other was his knowledge of the whereabouts of the vial that he had given to Allie.

CHAPTER 27

To Know His Name

What was he looking at? There was no sound, and his eyes were trying to tell his mind what he saw. There was no color. There seemed to be slightly different shades of white that constantly blended into one blur. His eyes shifted his sight to one side and then the other. It looked like a huge flat white desert. But how could that be? His eyelids felt heavy and unyielding, and so he allowed them to fall shut. The immediate sense of relief washing over him told him that was a good move, and so he allowed the blackness that his eyes sent to his brain to dominate the moment.

He was not aware that time passed. He was not aware that his human form had not moved. He was not aware. Then slowly, like the rising of the ocean tide that steadily inches toward the shoreline, he could feel a tiny flick of movement deep within himself. His body wanted to move. The feeling grew and bubbled up until he was forced to send messages to his arms and legs so that he could push himself up. At first, nothing happened. And so, he rested. Then, as if totally on their own, his legs jerkily spasmed, and his fingers began to tingle, sending signals to his brain to slowly form a fist. Suddenly, his eyelids lifted, and his eyes opened wide with the knowledge that he was now awake. And aware.

He realized he was on the floor and the white desert in his vision was the ceiling. He did not remember how or when his body found itself on the floor, but there he was. His brain telegraphed that he had fallen, letting him understand why he was on the floor. He wanted to just close his eyes and let the blackness wash over him, but his brain screamed at him to move. Then another thought from his brain told him it would just be easier to slowly sink down toward oblivion where there would be silence and no pain.

He started the descent but then, from somewhere deep within his human will to live, he fought against that choice. He was not ready to give in. He was not ready to die. Somehow, he would find the strength, and so he willed the muscles in his legs to work. At first, nothing happened. But then, as if they were guided by a separate will, his legs contracted, and his arms and his core joined in the rising effort, and he brought himself up on one elbow. It was exhausting. He was aware that he could easily fall back if he paused, and so he closed his eyes, and with every bit of strength within his being, he pulled into a sitting position.

His head was bowed down and felt as if it weighed one hundred pounds, but his brain was suddenly filled with an energy that urged him to continue to move, and so he did. He was close to a table leg, and he instinctively leaned against it. Its solidness gave him the strength to continue. He tucked his legs underneath himself and rolled to one side, pulling himself away from the floor. He was slowly rising, but it felt as if gravity reached up and pulled him back. This sudden falling motion attacked his mind with an instant fear that he must not stop. It was a now-or-never realization, and so he became a single unit telling himself to rise.

His eyes closed, and his body commanded itself to work toward standing. To get up. And then, without knowing how he did it, he got up. His legs were supporting him, but just barely, and he knew they would soon give way. He twisted his torso slightly and pushed himself toward a chair. It seemed like forever, but he felt himself falling through space, and then he crashed. But he had guessed right, and he came to a sudden, painful stop in a chair. He was not breathing, and his lungs screamed for air, so he gasped, felt the wonder of oxygen flooding into his chest, and his mind cleared, and he felt the exhilaration of winning.

He was up. He lowered his head, closed his eyes, and stayed very still. He could hear his breath move in and out of his body, and he thanked his belief in a higher power. He thanked God. And he rested. Time passed. And then he heard a sound. It was a sound he knew, but what was it? And then he knew, and he felt a laugh erupt from his throat. His stomach was gurgling. It was that gurgling sound telling him he needed to eat. He was hungry. Apparently, his world was wanting to function on a normal level, and he needed food. Gingerly, he sat up straight and pulled his legs and his arms toward himself with the grateful knowledge that this movement was pain-free.

But then he raised his head, and a stabbing pain seared from behind his eyes, filling his head with a white-hot light. His breath caught in his throat, and he heard a moaning sound. He was not aware he was making the sound as he fought the spinning sensation of the room moving around him. It felt as if he was falling, but he found he was gripping the chair with a viselike hold that threatened to break his fingers. He tried to relax, but the laser-like pain was in control. If he gave in, he knew he would slowly sink back down to the floor, and so he willed his mind to find a place that he could safely exist and control his reactions.

He found that place. It was within his breath. He dialed into his breath. Breathe in. Breathe out. Breathe in. And this time, when you breathe out, feel your body. Feel and control the pain in your head. Be bigger than the pain. And so, he sat motionless. Breathing. And soon he knew he was in charge, and he was bigger than the pain. He had won. He lowered his head, and tears fell onto his arms. He let his tears come, and he cried until the tears fell no more.

Lenny was going to be all right. He had slipped and fallen and hit his head, but he had not given in to the trauma, and he would eventually be all right. But at that moment, he did not even know where he was and, what was even worse, who he was. The pain was threatening to overtake his remaining strength, and so he rested in the chair and waited. He had won. Just barely. But Lenny had won.

*****

The Third understood Lenny's comfort level of being alone as he himself felt happiest when he was all by himself. However, it was different for him because he was surrounded by the closeness of people who lived in his building. Lenny did not have that surrounding human protection. Lenny lived totally alone—alone in a house within a stone's throw of the Arctic Circle in a little town called Kensington. Really alone. And so The Third worried.

The Third had made the decision it had been necessary to send Allie northward to deliver the vial to Lenny. The Third knew that it was a truly dramatic, if not drastic, decision, but at the time, he could not think of another way to get the vial to Lenny. He did not feel that Allie would be under any danger transporting the vial and its contents, so it would be an adventure for her. And it would mean the vial would be safely delivered.

Still, he was not happy, and he hated that he had to use his friendship with Allie to get the vial to its destination at Lenny's home. This fact gave The Third a terrible stress and an ever-increasing headache, and so he gave in and sank back into the comfort of the couch that was always willing to serve his needs.

And so, it was that The Third considered his decision a win-win situation even as his mind plunged into darkness as sleep overtook him.

CHAPTER 28

Nothing Is Ever Simple

Lennie had been able to stand and stagger his way to the bathroom where he unceremoniously inhaled two Advil pills and washed the cut on his head and applied a butterfly bandage. He looked at his image in the mirror and suddenly realized he did not know who he was looking at. What was his name? It was absurd that he did not know, and the harder he tried, he found he drew a blank. He barely recognized the face that stared back at him from the mirror, which made it more painful as he fought the all-encompassing headache. He wanted to sleep. But something told him that he was at a desperate place, having fallen, and if he slept, he might not wake up.

The room once again began to spin, and he could feel his stomach announce it was about to erupt and lose its contents, and so he bent over the toilet, and the sound of retching filled his bathroom as muscle spasms reigned supreme. His head continued to ache, but at least the spinning stopped, so he slowly lowered himself down to sit on the toilet.

Once secure, he allowed his mind to open itself to his situation, and he found he was scared. Really scared. It was not a new feeling for Lenny but one that he had pushed far back into his subconscious and a feeling that he rarely had to acknowledge in his adult life. But now he felt singular, unadulterated fear. Being a pragmatic person, he decided to take stock of what he did know.

He did know he had a horrendous headache, and he smiled at that realization and spoke aloud to himself and said, "Duh." First point. Have headache. Then he realized he must have fallen and that he was in his own home. He looked around hoping that it would all look familiar. It did not. It just looked like any average bathroom. He shook his head and instantly cried out in pain as a lightning-like pain bounced around inside his head. He instinctively sent both hands to his forehead as if to hold his scalp together.

Second point. Do not shake head. His mind raced. Name. What the hell was his name? He had never felt such a debilitating, sinking feeling. Not being able to know his own name. He should call for help. He knew there was a phone number that you dialed when you needed assistance. He did not know the number. Apparently, that number was in the same memory bank as his name, and both drew blanks. He wanted to laugh at the absurdity of it all. Cannot remember name. Need number to get help. Cannot remember number. Cannot remember name or number. Suddenly, a string of curse words came from his mouth. Lenny smiled. It seemed he could remember those words.

Think. Think logically. He must be in his own home, so somewhere there must be paperwork. Point three. Mind still trying to work. Good sign. Paperwork will not be in the bathroom, and there must be a den or an office, which means standing up to walk there. He put one hand on his knee and reached up and grasped the sink and took a deep breath and willed himself to stand. It was a tremendous effort, and his entire body screamed as he ever so slowly rose to his full height. He looked in the mirror and was stunned by his color or lack of it. He was white. So white he was almost a shade of light green. And he looked scared. His eyes telegraphed fear that said he was lost in his own home. How drastic was that?

He stood, still grateful that the room was not spinning, but he instinctively knew he might not have the strength to stand for long, so he tested his balance and moved one foot toward the door. Then he moved his other foot, and in slow motion, he moved his body forward and told his mind to concentrate on balance. Two more steps and he was at the bathroom door. Two more steps and he was through the door, moving toward a place to find out what his name was. It felt unreal, but he knew he had to stay alert and in control over this unbelievable situation.

When push came to shove, Lenny was most capable of dealing with handling an unexpected calamity, and so he moved forward with a robot-like precision.

His entire being focused on his need to exist. His need to know his name.

CHAPTER 29

The Innocent Lambs

Allie felt the wheels of the plane caress the runway as the weight of the plane welcomed the gravity of earth. The sudden and high screaming whine of the engines as the pilot threw them into reverse to slow the speed of the plane was the sweetest song she had ever heard. She was suddenly aware that she had been holding her mind and her body in a vise so tight that it was painful to move. She felt the speed of the plane slow in the landing, and she equally felt herself relaxing. She was amazed to find she was literally sinking back into her seat. She closed her eyes and let the "thankful feeling" wash over her as her mind accepted the fact that they had safely landed.

She looked across the aisle and smiled into the eyes of her new friend and was suddenly famished and found she was looking forward to their sharing a meal in the comfort of the airport terminal.

Back at Whispering Palms, The Third found himself thinking clearly for the first time in what seemed like forever. He allowed his mind to explore this new place—a place where he was able to move his thoughts through the past months as if he was speed-reading through a book. It was as if a movie was unfurling in his brain, and he marveled at watching and acknowledging the storyline.

It was all there. He saw his father, The Second, arriving at his laboratory and scooping him away to live at Whispering Palms. He saw his experiments fail. And then fail again. And then finally succeed beyond all his imaginations. He marveled at his friendship with

Allie, and he shuddered when he realized he had sent her, with the vial, to meet with his friend Lenny. It was at this point that he realized the immenseness of the situation.

The unknown men who were constantly following him would most certainly know of his association with Allie and were, most likely, following her. Why hadn't he thought of this sooner? He could not breathe, and he felt his entire being scream out that he could no longer allow the events to continue to go forward without intervening.

Allie was in danger, and he had put her there. And what was even worse was that he could not reach Lenny. Had he put him in danger as well? If these men following him were as good as he thought they must be, they would know of his association with Lenny. The Third was not worried about his own safety; however, his mind took stock of what he had done in his attempt to make certain the vial was in good hands.

In his attempt to confuse the men who constantly followed him, he had put Allie and now apparently Lenny in danger. He knew Lenny possibly better than Lenny knew himself, and he had used his friendship with him for the protection of the vial. And he had done the same with Allie. In doing this, he thought he was being smarter than these men. These men who probably killed without a second thought.

Cold shivers ran the length of his body, and he could feel the goosebumps of cold giving way to the layers of heat that ran the length of his body. He was not smarter than these criminals, and he had probably led them to the only two humans he liked and trusted—Allie and Lenny.

It was the first time in his life that he wanted to die. In his core, he truly wanted to die, but in his heart, he could not just give up and let the wolves stalk the innocent lambs. The innocent lambs were his friends who he had unknowingly introduced to his enemies—the wolves. If he did nothing, he would be as bad as the men who had stalked him and now were probably stalking the only two friends whom he had in this world.

What had he done? Indeed. What had he done!

CHAPTER 30

Inner Strength

The atmosphere inside the plane, as it gradually turned itself from the end of the runway to slowly roll toward the safety and warmth of the airport terminal, could best be described as jubilant as the passengers realized they had somehow survived a midair tragedy.

Each person silently sent their blessings and thanks toward the captain who had brought them back to earth unscathed. Their stories, as they later described the flight to their families and friends, would wildly differ from that of a small airborne happening to a near-death adventure where they were inches from meeting death in the air. Most were on their phones dialing loved ones to tell them they had indeed arrived and how the flight had shown them how grateful they were to be back safely on planet Earth. Mortal man becomes most willing to talk to other humans when they have been shown that they are, indeed, a hairbreadth away from meeting their Maker.

Allie found she was anxious to leave this airplane cabin, and she busied herself gathering her belongings. Her mind, during this episode, had been on her beloved cat, Oreo. She loved the unconditional love she received from her feline roommate. She closed her eyes and found she could feel the warmth and softness of his coat from memory. She loved how she always felt when he curled himself up beside her and awarded her attention with the glorious sound of purring that came from deep within him.

Allie had always wondered if he knew that the sound of purring was telling her that he loved her as his human. She shook her head at this thought, realizing that she was projecting her human feelings onto an animal, expecting it to understand and return her need for love. She did admit that she missed Oreo terribly and silently vowed to give him all manner of tender loving care once she was back in her home.

The voice of the flight attendant cut into her reverie, and Allie realized that while she would probably never again fly their airline, she was grateful they had deposited her safely at her destination. She suddenly realized a voice was headed her way, and she looked across the aisle to see Blake intently speaking in her direction.

"I'm sorry, Blake, I can't hear what you're saying," she said with a sharpness that surprised even herself, and so she tempered her statement with the suggestion that they talk once they had left the plane. He nodded his understanding and turned back toward his seat and busied himself gathering up his belongings.

There is a universal happening that occurs upon all airplanes once they have reached their destinations, and the passengers are allowed to stand and rescue their belongings. No one speaks. The clicking sound of the overhead bins as they open is the only sound in the cabin until the captain mercilessly beams music through the speakers.

It is our childhood training from school when we are taught to stand and wait in line that takes effect as each passenger patiently waits for their turn to move up the aisle to leave the plane. People greeting each other reminds each one that they have successfully completed their long airplane journey and are grateful to finally be at their destinations.

Allie made a beeline for the ladies' restroom, and she stood before one of the sinks and looked into the mirror. She decided she did not look too bad, considering what she had gone through, and she quickly ran her fingers through her hair to try to gently tease it back into place. She rummaged through her purse to find some lipstick and a comb. When one of the stalls became free, she gratefully moved into it.

She thought about possibly trying to use her cell phone to contact The Third but decided against it as his last words were not to contact him until she had turned the vial over to his friend Lenny. She did, however, have Lenny's phone number, so she decided she would call him after her meal with Blake. She suddenly realized that she was quite hungry, and so the sooner she stepped out into the terminal, the sooner she would be ordering and enjoying food.

She shook her head in quiet amazement as she realized that she had indeed found her appetite during these travels. Allie was not ruled by food as some people are and often forgot to eat lunch while at work. It was not a smart habit, she knew, but somehow the traveling introduced her to the joy of eating. Perhaps it is because you almost feel trapped as you find yourself waiting in lines in a terminal, and you cannot wander over to a handy refrigerator and satisfy your hunger.

It is a bit of a human element to want what you want when you want it, and traveling takes that privilege away, at least while you are making your way to your destination. She took one last look at herself in the mirror, and she straightened her slightly rumpled clothing and decided she passed muster.

Okay, she thought, *let us go and have some food and hopefully some enjoyable dialogue with Blake.* Her hand went to the vial that nestled against her chest. After eating, she would contact The Third's friend Lenny to tell him she was in Seattle and when her flight for Kensington would be leaving so he could meet her when she arrived.

Allie felt a quiet feeling overtaking her mind of almost accomplishing her trip to make sure that this vial with its precious contents be delivered safely to The Third's scientist friend, Lenny. Allie would not know that Lenny was suffering a bout of amnesia after his fall, and he was not one to trust anyone even when he knew his own name, and now he was even more of a recluse.

In life, it's a good thing we cannot see what the future holds in store for any of us, or Allie would not have so offhandedly thought that her journey with the vial was almost at an end. Out in the airport terminal, two men waited for her to emerge from the ladies' room, and one was Blake and the other was a man who was following them both.

The Mexican sat on a bench in the airport terminal, trying to look as if he was reading a newspaper. He had not counted on Allie being with anyone as she had been traveling alone. Now this extra person added a huge obstacle to his assignment of getting the vial from her. While staring blankly at his newspaper, his mind was clicking along on how to proceed. He thought of calling his contact, but he knew they would not know anything about this male she was with because he had watched them meet when they were in the airplane cabin.

Nothing is ever simple, he thought to himself. She was an attractive lady, and it was obvious this man she had met on the plane was doing his best to cater to her every need. Shaking his head, he marveled at how humans, men and women, were forever seeking the company of the other. His mind went to his wife who had no idea he was connected to the Mexican mafia. She thought he was a traveling insurance salesman. At the beginning of their marriage, she had attempted to be interested in his travels, but he had made his explanations to her so boring that she soon lost interest. Neither had wanted children, and his wife had established her own network of clubs she belonged to, and the news of them were equally boring to him, and so, within their marriage, they traveled their separate ways.

She would not know of his extracurricular business, and he would not know of her extracurricular affairs as she found the men in these clubs eager and willing to have on-the-side sexual encounters. She marveled at how most men did not give the fact that they were cheating on their wives a second thought. There was something very safe in an affair one has within their marital life because each person did not want their spouses to know of their indiscretions. There was a kind of ironclad protection built around the affair. It was understood that they did not want to leave their marriages and only desired to cheat on their spouses while exploring the newness of another person.

Usually, these wanderings did not last long as the sexual conquest was over soon, and when the discovery of the new partner became too familiar, both partners would find a way to end the affair. It was a sad acknowledgment that most people no longer accepted that being faithful was part of the modern marriage agreement. Most had been married a few years and were childless, and each had their own careers in full swing. Once children would enter their lives, this way of life would change.

Until then, they would continue to take part in this dance of leading two separate sexual lives.

CHAPTER 31

I'm Here. You're Not

"Well, I am here, and you are not," the Mexican growled into the phone, unsuccessfully trying to hide the impatient sound of his voice. "She is no longer alone and is planning to have a meal with the man she met on the plane. I am telling you that I need to make my move now. Now, while she is still alone."

The Mexican had decided that he would be making his move even if his contact did not give him the go-ahead. His discipline to always advise the man-in-charge took over, and so he had been on his phone calling them from the airport terminal.

He had watched Allie go into the ladies' room, and so he had stationed himself a few feet to the left of the entrance so he could see when she came out. His breathing was shallow, and he could sense the familiar feeling he always experienced when he was about to close in on a suspect.

The voice on the other end of the phone was silent. The Mexican dutifully waited, and finally the voice spoke. "I will trust your judgment" was all the voice said, and the click of the dial tone told the hit man all that he needed to know. He had been given free rein to do anything he had to within his assignment of Allie and the vial.

Another man was also pretending to be on his phone, and he was sitting at a table, reserving a space for Allie. He had a clear view of the restroom door. Blake did not need to check in with his superior. If he had his way, Allie would not have had a chance to disappear from his view, but he was an excellent actor, and his calm exterior did not show his interior stress level. Blake was battling a different emotion as he found himself really liking Allie. He had thoroughly enjoyed their conversations while they were in the airplane. He sighed as this was not a time for normality, so he continued to appear as if he was enthusiastically working the crossword puzzle in his newspaper as he waited for Allie to come out of the restroom.

Unbeknownst to Allie, she had two men whose sole purpose was to keep her in their sights because she had the vial hanging around her neck.

CHAPTER 32

Time to Be an Adult

The Third was bordering on panic mode. He could not reach Lenny. He should not reach out to Allie, and he did not want to reach out to his father, which meant he was all alone, and it was time to be an adult and make some grown-up decisions.

The walls of his apartment were closing in on him, and he paced the small length of his living room. He had ventured out to get a few groceries and had spotted the dark van that was parked just outside the entrance to his building. He instinctively knew that it contained men who were there to watch him and his movements. He could not call the police. He would not call his father. He was all alone.

Strangely, that knowledge gave The Third the inner strength that he needed. He stopped his pacing and slowly sat down on his couch. He would have loved to just sit back and disappear into the soft comfort of the cushions and turn his mind off, but he knew that Allie would need him to be strong. He made a list in his mind to make flight arrangements to go north to Lenny's. He thought he had about $10,000 in cash safely hidden in his apartment. He had, over the years, acquired clothing suitable for the Arctic temperatures. He also had several passports in various names, and he even had a small handgun, although he had never had the chance to learn how to use it.

He silently cursed himself for involving Lenny. He loved Lenny, but he had known for most of his lifetime that Lenny was deficient.

Deficient in his ability to handle everyday matters. Lenny was brilliant as a scientist, but like many scientists, he lacked the ability to function with a common-sense attitude. The Third had always known this, and so he had always intended to get some help for Lenny. He knew that Lenny had a temper when he was faced with everyday solutions that he was supposed to follow involving other human beings. It was the reason that he lived just shy of the Arctic Circle. It was a place that he could survive on his own without having to deal with society.

The Third had always known the day would come when he would have to step up and be the adult in the room, but now, Lenny was AWOL. Where was he? Was he all right? Is his being missing due to a function of something that he did himself or something that someone did to him? It was bad enough that the men in the van lurking outside The Third's building were stalking him. Did they somehow know about Lenny?

The Third suddenly stopped pacing, acutely aware of the throbbing of his head and the pain that was working its way down his neck to his shoulders. He stood still and felt as if he were like the weather vane that reached up into the sky, daring the lightning to strike it. He worried that the pain would overtake his entire body, rendering him useless. He wanted to do something useful. But his mind and body were weak when it came to pain, and he sank slowly onto the couch, reaching for the bottle of pills. He hated himself for swallowing the handful of pills, but he could not fight nor stop the desire.

His mind, still alert, brought the vision of Lenny up on the inside of his brain. He saw his friend so clearly, and he could taste the knowledge that he needed to—he needed to—his vision of Lenny was slowly disappearing as The Third was losing his ability to act both physically and mentally. He surrendered once again to the lure of the couch as it once again allowed him to collapse in a virtual puddle of nothingness.

Lenny did indeed need The Third's help, but Lenny was in his own private hell and could not remember who he was, let alone who The Third was. The two scientists had both been subject to a present lobotomy of sorts, and their brilliant minds were silenced—at least for the time being.

*****

Allie felt a surge of energy and purpose return after her visit to the comfort of the ladies' room. There is something about being able to reach out to one's body to refresh it after a period of being confined. The pure act of splashing water onto one's face, running a comb through one's hair, and rearranging clothing do wonders, and Allie experienced that wonder. She knew she was tired and was fighting a feeling of stress that she could not identify, and her body was screaming for food, but over and above all these problems, Allie felt happy. Perhaps it was because she was no longer tied down to a passenger seat in an airplane. Or it could be she was feeling an ego surge having had a good-looking, young man apparently anxious to please her. It did not matter to Allie. She reveled in the joy of feeling good. She stood taller and put on a welcoming smile as she walked toward the exit of the ladies' room, out into the hustle and bustle of the airport terminal.

As Allie strode out of the ladies' restroom, Blake immediately stood and raised his hand holding the newspaper and waved in her direction. Allie immediately saw his motion and moved toward him with a smile. Blake caught his breath as he watched her come toward him. He could not ignore how beautiful she appeared and how he felt a warm glow move through his body in anticipation of being able to once again be close to her. His mind knew he should stop this feeling, but his body refused, and so he relaxed and let the feeling wash over him. He would enjoy the next hour or two being in the presence of this gorgeous female. Later he would be strong and do whatever he had to do to complete his assignment. For now, he would enjoy her presence. He reached out his hand and took hers, and together they turned and walked toward the airport restaurant.

Curse words erupted in the mind of the Mexican who was closely watching Allie and Blake walk together toward the restaurant. He had missed his chance to get Allie alone, and now she was with another person, making his chance to successfully complete his mission twice as difficult. But he had faced many other situations that had appeared headed for failure, and his tenacity and his greed for money had always given him successful outcomes. This time he was determined it would be no different.

Allie was just another situation that he would meet head-on and find a way to succeed no matter what he had to do to make it happen.

CHAPTER 33

Where Are You?

Jim picked up the phone. He had dialed the local police department. "Yes, I'd like to file a missing persons report," he heard himself say. The headache was beginning to form again as it always did every time Jim was faced with the fact that one of his employees was missing. The person on the other end of the phone, with a bored-sounding voice, was asking for the particulars, which Jim could, by now, recite without checking any paperwork.

Where on earth are you? he asked himself silently. Allie was the last person, the last employee that he could imagine would go missing. Jim had hoped that during the time since Allie had not reported for work, someone—a girlfriend, a family member, a neighbor, anyone—would come forward and present him with a reasonable explanation as to her disappearance. One often read in the newspaper or heard on the news of people missing; however, never in his years would Jim have imagined that he would be one of those people having to file a missing persons report.

The "bored voice" on the phone informed him that they would put this missing persons report into their system, and they would let him know if, or when, they had any information pertaining to missing persons report number MP3270188, and was there anything else he needed?

Jim knew that to ask when he might hear from them was a lost cause because of the way the bored voice sounded, but he could not help himself. He had to ask. "Can you give me a timetable as to when you might have some information?" he said, and his headache was now in full bloom. The bored voice said exactly what Jim had expected, telling him there was not a set time frame and that they would contact him when they heard anything.

Jim hung up without saying "thank you" or "goodbye," which was totally out of character for him, but his headache was ruling his attitude. He opened his desk drawer to get an aspirin for his full-blown headache. He hesitated and then took two pills and swallowed them without any water. He was beginning to have an uneasy feeling in the pit of his stomach that his best employee might be in more trouble than he could imagine. He slowly opened the folder on his desk that read "Allie Birks" and made a notation of the missing persons report. Jim sighed as he began the schedule of his workday knowing it would be a long day. *Where are you, Allie?* he thought. *Where on earth are you?*

When Allie had decided that she would help The Third and deliver his vial to his friend, Lenny, there had not been any time to go to Jim's office to tell him of her decision. It had all happened so fast that she barely had time to throw a few changes of clothing into a suitcase and then accept the money and tickets from The Third. She drove her car to the airport with The Third riding in the passenger seat and parked it in the long-term parking lot. She gave The Third her ticket and instructed him to hold it for her until she returned. Allie felt that was the safest thing to do as she would be traveling, and he would be back in his apartment at Whispering Palms. From the long-term parking lot, Allie called a taxi, which picked them up and drove them to the airport terminal.

Once in the taxi, Allie realized she needed to let her boss, Jim, know where she had gone, so she wrote a short note for The Third to give it to Jim once he was back in his apartment. It was a good plan, and Allie had no reason to think that Jim would never receive her note. And The Third did have the note when he was in the taxi riding back to Whispering Palms; however, on their arrival, the taxi driver got out of his taxi and walked around it to open the rear seat door for his passenger. The Third had not expected this act of kindness, and it surprised him. When the taxi driver opened the rear door and reached in to help The Third out onto the sidewalk, he dropped the note, and it slipped underneath the taxi. Neither The Third nor the driver realized what had happened, and Allie's note to her boss, Jim, would never reach him.

*****

While Allie and Blake were enjoying a meal at the airport, neither were aware that they were under surveillance by the lone man who was determined to get the vial from Allie, and he was losing patience. He was used to quick assignments where he would be given instructions and he would decide how to proceed and would do it quickly. No one watched over him, and he had full control over his actions.

Usually, it meant that he would scope out the area and the comings and goings of the person to be disposed of, and then he would step out of the shadows with a knife with a long, thin stiletto blade. The knife had been his father's, and he cherished it because it held his family history. He was deadly accurate and could inflict a death blow so swiftly that most of his subjects did not know what happened. As they fell to the ground, he would take their picture as his proof of having accomplished the deed. He was good at his profession, and working alone in this manner had served him well over the years.

But now, with this assignment, he found that he was not able to quickly accomplish the killing. He was not comfortable in having to constantly keep Allie in sight but not step in and use his beloved knife. He was not comfortable in having to check in with the cartel bosses to receive further instructions. And now that another person, in the form of Blake, had entered the picture, he really was not comfortable. He desperately wanted to find a way to either step up and eliminate Allie, or inform the cartel that he was no longer their man. And yet he knew that his being uncomfortable was something he would have to endure. One did not go against the cartel no matter how uncomfortable you felt. And so, he swallowed his pride and decided he would make this assignment worth his while, and if that meant sticking with Allie and her newfound male friend, so be it. He would be like a glue that would stick to itself and would eventually find the way to make this discomfort pay out.

Allie would never know of his hatred or of his decision to somehow, sometime find the chance to use his beloved stiletto knife to silence her forever. The vial would be the goal to show the cartel of his brilliance, and he was certain it would mean he would advance in the standings within the underground organization. That fact alone gave him the willingness to continue stalking Allie, and so he took a deep breath and settled in to do whatever this assignment would demand of him.

*****

Blake chose a table that was toward the back of the restaurant and almost secluded, facing the entrance, as this was his training to always be in control of his surroundings. Allie could not know this, but she was grateful for the privacy and the ability to speak in a quiet tone. She was amazed at how she immediately felt a warm comfort level in his presence. It was as if she had known him all her life. This was one of Blake's accomplishments—to be able to put another person at ease. It had served him well; however, he found with Allie that he did not have to enact this training when they were together. If he had been more aware, he would have realized that he was already experiencing the beginning of the willingness to care deeply for someone of the opposite sex.

Throughout the meal, they relaxed and talked easily, exchanging the kind of conversation that most humans use when they are in the mode of getting to know someone. And so, Allie and Blake sat and chatted and found themselves in a sort of "bubble of togetherness" that would prove to protect and serve them in the future. One of the aspects of their conversation was that neither wanted to have to explain their reason for traveling. Blake, of course, knew of the vial that Allie carried around her neck, and Allie had no desire to speak of it.

So it remained the unspoken reason that they were together.

The Third had rested, and when he awoke, he found his mind was clear and ready to make whatever decision was necessary to help the two people he cared about—his long-time friend, Lenny, and his new friend, Allie.

He did not lapse into his usual frame of mind where he only thought of his own needs. Not being able to contact Lenny meant that something was very wrong. Sending Allie to give the vial to Lenny might mean that she would be walking into a dangerous situation, and so he would do whatever was necessary to find out why he could not reach Lenny and make certain Allie was safe.

CHAPTER 34

The Phone Rang and Rang

Lenny had succeeded in realizing that his recent fall in the bathroom had bounced his head off the tile floor hard enough to render him without the use of his memory. He moved toward the sink and ran some cold water, and using both hands, he splashed it over his face and head. It was jarring, but it felt good, and so he did it again, and then he felt his mind begin to function. He still did not know who he was, but he was certain he was in his own home, and so he knew he could find paperwork that would give him clues to his situation.

He wondered if he was married. Did he have children, or was he alone in this house? His brain felt exhilarated with the ability or the need to think, and so he wondered what he did with his life. Did he have a career, and if so, what was it? He was suddenly overcome with the realization that he literally knew nothing about himself, and this fact was almost debilitating; however, his scientist training kicked in, and he decided to find out one thing at a time. He would build his memory beginning with small facts until his concussion would give way, allowing him to regain his full memory.

Lenny was unique in his way as most people might have given in to panic at the realization of a lost memory; however, Lenny viewed it as a scientific challenge. He stood still for a moment, and then moving with a robot-like gait, he pointed himself to leave the bathroom to find himself somewhere within the walls of this house. He had the vague thought that someone would be coming to see him, and this feeling gave him comfort.

As a scientist, he made a mental note to document how it felt to be without name or knowledge, and then he slowly moved to leave the bathroom and explore the house. He grinned and relished the feeling of excitement that came with beginning an adventure. Lenny might not know who he was or what he did, but his mind could still learn and function, and this gave him the strength to move out into the world that was his house. He moved with a purpose of energy, allowing him to send his body forward to learn about himself. This was something new and unique, and he welcomed the challenge.

Suddenly, he could hear a phone ringing, and he was so grateful, realizing that whoever was calling him knew who he was, and so he moved with laser-like intent toward the sound of the phone. *Please, please keep ringing,* he thought. *Do not hang up. I am coming as fast as I can.* The ringing of the phone filled his being, and he moved toward the sound.

On the other end of the phone, The Third was impatiently willing Lenny to answer his phone. The Third had realized that this phone number was the only contact he had with Lenny, and he chided himself for not insisting that Lenny get a cell phone, as well as the landline into his home. He had mentioned it once to Lenny during one of their many conversations, but Lenny had immediately put down the suggestion of a second phone. He pointed out that he was rarely away from the house, and he simply did not need the expense of having a second phone.

The Third was holding his cell phone as it rang and rang, and the sound was like a loud, insistent voice that kept screaming out for Lenny to answer. The Third let the rings pile up as he tried to think why Lenny was not answering. Putting aside the panic thoughts of why he could not answer, The Third forced his mind to consider that Lenny might have driven into town to do the few errands in his schedule. He knew he would occasionally go to a grocery store to buy food to last for a few weeks, and he often stopped by the library to check out books as he was an avid reader. He had complained to The Third that the small-town library did not stock the advanced reading material that Lenny enjoyed. He had mentioned that he occasionally drove to a city to use the library in the area that offered a larger selection. The Third had suggested that he could use his computer to sign into the library and view and read books online, but Lenny had immediately quashed this suggestion saying he preferred to be able to hold the books in his hands.

The truth was that Lenny did not want to admit that he had not learned how to access this function of the library, and while The Third had guessed this was the situation, he had chosen not to let Lenny know. The Third had thought that one day in the future, when he would be able to visit Lenny in his far north home of Kensington, he would find a way to show Lenny the advantages of the online library features.

As he held the phone in his hand, listening to its incessant ringing, he wished that he had helped his friend sooner. He made a mental note to do this as soon as he could reach Lenny. In the meantime, the phone he held rang and rang and rang.

In Lenny's home, the phone rang and rang and rang, and he slowly made his way from the bathroom to the room where the ringing was coming from. It took all his concentration to move and not fall, and he silently willed the phone to continue ringing. He was within a few feet of the phone, and he reached out to pick it up when the ringing stopped. All he heard when he lifted the headset was the sound of the dial tone as it seemed to be brutally saying, "You are too late! You missed it. You are too late!" With a fury he did not know he possessed, he slammed the receiver down on the phone with such a violent motion that he was surprised the phone did not shatter. Swear words filled the air as he vented his anger. He was coming to answer it. He was doing his best to answer it. It should have waited for him to get there.

He felt as if all the air from his body was evaporating, and afraid he might fall again, he moved toward a nearby chair and collapsed into it. Suddenly, without his permission, tears erupted and cascaded down his cheeks. He was doing his best to answer the phone. It was not fair. He had desperately needed to answer the phone to find out who had called him so that they could tell him who he was. The overwhelming aloneness washed over him like a sudden rainstorm, and he sat still in the chair and cried and cried.

And the phone sat silent watching him cry.

CHAPTER 35

The Unknown Man

Allie and Blake sat at the table long past the time when they had finished their meal. Each one silently wished they could stay longer and relish in the enjoyment they felt in being with the other. Blake had paid for the meal and included a tip far beyond the usual with the understanding given to the waiters that they were not to be disturbed. Waiters in airport restaurants were used to people who were in between flights who would use the table as a place to pass the time. If it was not a rush hour when they needed the tables, and especially if the tip reflected the need of the person to stay there, they did not press for them to leave.

During the meal, Blake had noticed a lone man at a table with a view of their table, and he recognized him from their flight. It might be a coincidence in the coming and going of travelers, or as Blake's experience would tell him, he might be following them. He knew, if he was following them, he was following Allie and probably for the same reason Blake had been assigned to follow her. He needed to find out about the precious vial she carried and better yet, to find out where she was taking it. Blake resolved that when they parted company, he would follow Allie, watching to see if that lone man was also following her. If that was the case, he felt that Allie was in danger.

The Mexican underworld often crossed paths with Blake as their interests usually consisted of the same situations and people. While Blake had been given instructions to find out the designation and person to whom the vial would be delivered, he was certain the Mexican following her would not consider her safety.

For this reason alone, Blake had vowed he would drop back when they parted and see if the man would go his own way or if he would continue to follow Allie. He did not want any harm to come to her, and if he had to, he would go against the unknown man lurking at the nearby table.

Blake had walked Allie to the concourse gate where her flight was to take off. She had just under an hour, and while he had offered to stay with her, she said she did not want to take up more of his time, and so he did not insist. He needed the time to scope out the area and see if that man was still following Allie. It was a little awkward when they said goodbye, as a handshake was too formal, and yet a kiss was too intimate; and so Blake had settled for a quick adult-type hug. He was somewhat stunned by how the closeness of this woman sent a cascade of chills down his frame, and he wanted to reach out and hold her against him.

Allie also reacted with a physically exciting response to his touch; however, she shook it off as the sadness of seeing someone leave whom you felt a growing closeness with because of the company. Being alone in traveling a great distance was not something she had a lot of experience with. She noted that Blake seemed to easily say goodbye, and so she told herself to do the same thing.

The small airline flying the final leg north to Kensington posted a delay of thirty minutes, and Allie thought about calling the phone number The Third had given her of Lenny. Then she realized he would be getting the same information at the Kensington airport, so she found herself once again looking for a ladies' restroom. She chuckled to herself that she seemed to be taking a tour of all the restrooms in the different airports. She was beginning to sense a bit of fatigue from the hours of traveling and decided that splashing some cold water on her face would work wonders. She was grateful that this trip was close to its end, and she would be heading home to her adorable cat. The thought of Oreo flooded her mind as she headed toward the sign advertising the ladies' restroom.

When Allie disappeared inside the restroom, the lone Mexican once again stationed himself so he could watch the door and Allie's movements. However, one flight above, in the airport's double-decker lobby, Blake was also watching Allie go into the restroom. He could see that the Mexican was following her. He picked up his phone to alert his handlers that they were to stand by in case he needed to call for a backup.

Allie was unaware that two men were watching her every move.

CHAPTER 36

A Contented Oreo

Whispering Palms now knew that their beloved Allie was not on vacation, and she was not ill; but worst yet, she was apparently missing as no one knew of her whereabouts. She had apparently been seen speaking with Mr. Freedman, and she had worked on that day, but after that, no one could say that they had seen her. A check of her apartment showed that she had not picked up her mail, and the apartment manager said that he had not had any paperwork from Allie stating that she would be away.

Her neighbor, Ms. Wilhelm, had said that she and Allie had an agreement to check on each other, and so, when she had heard Oreo meowing loudly during the night, she let herself in to feed Oreo. When she learned from Allie's employer that Allie seemed to be missing, she took Oreo into her apartment where he promptly curled up in her knitting basket and, having a full tummy, fell sound asleep. Ms. Wilhelm told Jim that she would be keeping Oreo until Allie returned. She also said this had never happened before, and she was certain it must be a family emergency, and Allie would be in touch with everyone as soon as possible.

Jim was not so sure it was as easy and cut-and-dried as that. It was so out of character for Allie not to let her friends and her employer know of her plans to be away. Jim had a strange, sinking feeling in his stomach as it had fallen to him to alert the police of a missing person. He found that the chore of filling out the missing person forms gave one a terrible sensation that not all was well with his employee. While Allie was an adult who always seemed to be in total control of her life, there was a naivety about her that Jim felt could possibly be sensed by anyone who was not so aboveboard. One often heard news reports about young women who suddenly went missing, and families would desperately ask the public if anyone knew of their whereabouts. Sometimes you would hear news reports that a young lady had been found murdered.

Jim shuddered at the thought this might happen to someone he knew. It bothered him so much that he picked up his phone and called his home to check on his family. His wife knew of the situation and assured him that everyone was safe and sound at home and that Allie probably was safe somewhere too. Her absence must be a misunderstanding and that she would contact everyone very soon.

Jim agreed with his wife but did not tell her of the sinking feeling that he had that something was very wrong. Jim's wife also had the same misgivings, but she wanted to spare her husband the worry about one of his favorite employees. As she hung up the phone, she felt the same sinking feeling that Allie would not have left without a note to Jim. The world was not as safe a place as it used to be, and missing young women always seemed to be in the evening news. It was just that they did not know those missing women.

Now they knew one, and it was Allie.

CHAPTER 37

Believe in Santa Claus

Lenny ran out of steam. He could no longer cry. He became aware of the silence of the room, and for some strange reason, that fact made him angry. He needed sound because that would fill the horrible void of amnesia that he found himself in. Sound in the room would help him think. He had never liked television; however, now he decided it would be his best friend for the moment. He took several deep breaths to steady himself so that he could stand. His head pounded, and angrily, he willed himself to ignore the pain. Slowly, ever so slowly, he concentrated on transferring his weight from his sitting position to his legs. It seemed like a horrendously difficult task, but once he began to use his muscles, he found he did have control of his body. It seemed like forever, but within a minute, he was standing up, and he could not have been prouder of himself. He pointed his body in the direction of the television. The invention that he had scorned and looked down on all these years would hopefully tell him some of the things he needed to know. What day was it? What year? What country was he in? Basic memories that we take for granted unless we find ourselves in a world that is totally blank. At least it was something, and it would be the tool he could use until his memory returned. Hopefully, whoever had been calling him on the phone would soon call back. Lenny made a mental note that once he was able to regain his memory, he would write down all the thoughts and feelings he was experiencing.

He was unaware that his scientific brain was functioning as it always had even though it did not remember his name.

*****

The Third was frustrated beyond belief as he had always been able to pick up a phone, and within a few moments, his friend Lenny's voice would come through the receiver loud and clear and ever reliable and present. And now, when he needed to speak to him, all he heard was the ringing of his phone.

The Third had taken the dramatic step of sending a young girl to Lenny, carrying the vial that contained the most precious of all fluids. Now it was as if he could feel a sinister presence. He did not need to feel a sinister presence. He needed to feel that everyone in his small world was all right and that the vial was safely delivered to his laboratory in Lenny's home.

He wanted to dial Lenny's number again but did not want to hear the incessant ringing with no answer, and so he would wait. He closed his eyes and wished he could send mental telepathy thoughts to his friend. While he knew it was not possible, he imagined his mind would have the strength to do just that. It was like that of a child who knew there really was no Santa Claus but wanted to believe in the fantasy anyway. The Third wanted Lenny to accept his thoughts so that they both could enjoy the illusion that all was right with their worlds.

*****

Lenny stood in front of the television. The boob tube was the slang term his generation had given it, and he decided it was well-earned as a seemingly endless array of commercials marched across the screen. His head hurt. His body hurt. Everything hurt, and here he stood listening to words spilling out into the room, inviting him to buy furniture polish, and ladies cosmetics, and fast cars, and on and on and on about the weather and then more commercials. When the news finally came on, Lenny found that he was no wiser as to his situation, but what he did realize was that the world itself was totally screwed up. Wars and famine and climate change. A lot about climate change. But nothing local. Lenny became acutely aware that he was indeed all alone in his world.

He suddenly was so thirsty he could hardly breathe, and he turned from the boob tube and shuffled forward to make himself move to another room. He passed through a door to find a room that was filled with test tubes and all manner of scientific apparatus. Charts hung from the walls, and a variety of test tubes showed there were ongoing experiments. *This is what I do?* he thought. But his knowledgeable mind remained absent, and all he could do was stare at the room.

Through a door across the expanse of the room, he could see a large white box, and while he could not recognize that it was a refrigerator, he decided it might be where he could find liquid. His mouth was so dry that his breath hurt when he reached for air, and so he carefully stumbled in the direction of the white box. As he moved, it was as if a flash of white lightning erupted inside his eyes, and he was fighting off the pain. He instinctively knew to steady himself so he would not collapse to the floor. But along with the flash of white light, he saw a man. It was only a very tiny picture, but it was as if his mind was a camera, and he could clearly see the image. He could not know that it was The Third, but the picture stayed with him. The image was so clear he felt as if he could reach out and touch it. Everything else was still a blank, but at least he had that one vision, and he was not going to let it go.

*****

The Third could not shake the overwhelming feeling of fear that washed over him, and so, with his hands shaking, he dialed a different number. He could not reach Lenny, and this was something he had not factored into the plan. Finally, the different number he had dialed began to ring. And it rang, and rang, and rang, and with each ring, a knot in his stomach grew larger and tighter. The fact that the person he was calling did not answer was a final assault to his nervous system. He was certain he would faint or throw up or do both at the same time. His legs gave way, and he sank to his knees, and he heard himself moan, "Oh no! Oh no!" The number he was dialing was to the cell phone he had given Allie. He had given her explicit instructions that she was to use it to call him if she needed help on her trip north to meet his friend Lenny. The Third was quite certain that no one knew she had the vial, and so she would not be in danger traveling alone. Giving her the phone was his way of creating a lifeline between them. And now, just like Lenny's phone, it just rang and rang and rang. He could not reach either of the two people whom he had allowed into his life and whom he considered friends.

Now The Third felt he had put them both in danger.

CHAPTER 38

A Place Where Humans Wait

He had finally decided that he would no longer wait until he made his move. Mexican people are not known for their patient ways. He had followed Allie all this way even when she was joined by a stranger, but now that stranger had left her alone, and so it was his time to make a move. The Seattle airport was a small one, at least compared to the huge terminals, and he had scouted their security and found it to be minimal. He would follow her until she was in a section of the airport that was sparsely populated, and he would approach her from behind. Using a small length of rope, he would use a kind of move used in rodeos to pull calves off their feet, and he would slam her to the ground. Throwing his weight on her upper body would further restrict her breathing and allow him to grasp the vial and wrench it away from her body. One last move would be to slam her head to the concrete to render her unconscious. As he thought about the action, his entire body felt a hot flush of adrenaline, and he could barely contain his pleasure.

*****

Allie had decided she would move through the main concourse and spend her time in the small section of the airport where her plane was scheduled to leave for Kensington. She wondered how it got its name. Kensington. Was it a family name? Who had chosen it? What was the population? She would use her phone to google the information. It would help her pass the time and give her something interesting to do. She was becoming a little tired of the traveling, and this would make the time pass faster.

One thing that can be said for every airport is that they are all similar in design and they all emit a sense of being aloof. They are not friendly, nor are they frightening. They are just—there. They are a place where humans wait. Patiently. In large and small groups. And everyone follows the unwritten rules not to intrude into another's space. It is this rule that was favorable to the Mexican trailing Allie and unfavorable to Allie herself.

Allie did not feel pain. She only felt a huge weight that was suddenly dragging her to the ground. And she could not breathe. It was as if she could not move and her mind and body retreated into a metamorphosis of a jumble of feelings. She saw light flashes. Her head seemed to scream inside. Her mind wanted her to fight back, but her body was paralyzed. She heard someone screaming but was not sure where the sound came from. The Mexican was indeed skilled in his ability to throw someone to the ground in a few seconds and stop them from any reaction to protect themselves.

The Mexican had his hand on the vial when, suddenly, he was hit from behind and thrown away from Allie's body. He had succeeded in breaking the chain, and while he found himself rolling over the concrete floor, he had the presence of mind to protect the vial with his body. He was not used to being attacked, and his animal sense of preservation kicked in, and he was able to get to his feet. He turned to see the body of Blake tackling him once more, and together they struggled as they fell to the floor. By chance, he fell on top of Blake, and by instinct, he jammed his fingers into Blake's face and eyes. In the next second, he jammed Blake's head into the floor, knocking him out, allowing him to tear himself away from the entanglement of their bodies. He crawled away and, finding a nearby concrete bench, was able to struggle up onto it and then stand. A crowd was forming around Allie and Blake who both lay unconscious on the gleaming walkway. He was able to slowly move backward until he found his balance. He stood for a millisecond to get his breath, and then he turned and quickly moved away from the crowd. He did not look back. The only sound was the incessant ringing of a phone that came from Allie's purse.

And it rang and rang and rang.

CHAPTER 39

No Answer

The Third decided he would wait no longer. He had tried many times to call Lenny, and there was no answer. He knew that the simple act of dialing again and again without a response was an act of futility, and so the time had come to reach out. He hated the thought, but even as his fingers pressed the cell phone numbers, he experienced feelings of relief. He knew he was calling someone who would help him because they had a lifetime of history. The phone was ringing, and finally a gruff voice answered, and Freedman Carver II was on the line with his son.

At first, his voice failed him because the sound of his father's voice always had the same effect. He became speechless. Finally, he said, "It's me." Each man knew the other's voice so well there was no need of any identification.

The Second hesitated, but he knew that his son would not have called him unless it was a dire situation, and so he simply said, "I'm here." The Third felt tears well up inside his heart, and for a moment, he was petrified that his father would hear him crying. With a tremendous effort, he controlled his voice and said, "I need some advice. And some help. Please."

The father had never heard his son utter such an intimate and needy statement, and his parental feelings told him to be strong and yet to show his son, by the sound of his voice, that he understood and was there for him. He needed only two words. "I understand," he said.

"I didn't mean for it to happen," said The Third. The father knew that the son had tried to do something meaningful, but it had not worked out. This was something of a pattern for the son, and the father had bailed him out many times before. Forgetting to pay bills. Letting his bank account fall below the minimum amount, or not keeping up with income taxes; and it was simply because The Third had absolutely no interest in monetary things. No amount of cajoling had managed to change him. So now he patiently waited to hear what the latest problem was.

The Second would find out how wrong his assumptions were and how much his son, The Third, really needed his help.

CHAPTER 40

A Handy-Dandy Time

The sunshine entered the room through the plate-glass window, making it even more assaulting in its brightness. It was as if it wanted to overtake the darkness of the hospital room, and it was saying, "Wake up! Get up! Move! You should not be here!" By virtue of their mere existence, all hospital rooms seem to generate the same atmosphere. It is a transient, not a homey, welcoming attitude because those who find themselves occupying a hospital room all have a singular wish and that is to leave.

And Allie would be no exception. She slowly opened her eyes and cautiously examined the space around her. It was white. Very white. White walls. White ceiling and white curtains surrounding a bed with white sheets. A harsh white light beamed from the ceiling. For a fleeting moment, it reminded Allie of the white fluffy clouds she had observed from the plane, wishing she could be enveloped in the whiteness. And now she was. She moved her head to explore the sight line, and a sudden lightning pain radiated across her chest, and she heard herself cry out. She immediately closed her eyes as if to protect herself from both the pain and all the whiteness. What she had seen told her she was probably in a hospital room, but what was she doing there? How did she get there? And why did she hurt so when she moved?

Humans are hardwired to know where they are always. When this information is not immediately forthcoming, the mind does a sort of "kamikaze dance," doing its best to orient its owner of its situation. It moves at breakneck speed going over the recent events, and this rapid action only serves to frustrate the human, which adds to the overall confusion.

Allie lay very still under the white covers, and she quietly took an inventory of the parts of her body that did not hurt. She found she could move her arms and legs, and though she was lying on her back, her torso was all right. It was just her head and her neck that violently sent spasms of pain through her being when she moved. Having completed her inventory, her hand went to her chest to find that the vial and the chain were not there. As if by unseen cue, a nurse came bustling in.

"Oh, good. You are awake," she said. "Welcome back to the real world. How do you feel?" She did not wait for an answer and continued with her one-sided conversation. "Never mind. I am sure you have a dandy headache, and I know those bruises on your neck hurt, so do not try to move too much. But we do need to get some water into you so that these handy-dandy pain pills will let you sit up without too much discomfort. Here, I will pour you a glass of water, and if you'll put these pills in your mouth, we'll have you feeling fine and dandy in no time."

Allie wondered how someone could so easily fit the words *handy-dandy* in one sentence so many times. When was the last time she had heard anyone use *handy-dandy* in a conversation? She took the water and the pills, and to her surprise, just the act of swallowing sent pain coursing through her body. A moan escaped as she let the liquid smoothly run down her throat, taking the "handy-dandy" pills to help with the pain.

The nurse said, "Just as I thought. You have a dandy bruise on your neck, and I am not surprised it hurts to swallow. It sure seems as if someone was hell-bent on mugging you. Imagine that happening at an airport? Who would have thought? Airports used to be so safe, but I guess they have their limitations too."

Allie attempted to force herself to talk to this nurse and only succeeded in making a pitiful croaking sound. The nurse said, "It's all right. You do not have to talk just now. It is best that you stay quiet and let the pills do their handy-dandy job of making you feel better. There is no reason on earth that you should have to be in pain when we can just pop two handy-dandy pain pills to have you feeling fine and dandy in no time." And with her handy-dandy diagnosis, the handy-dandy nurse bustled about Allie, tucking in sheets and plumping pillows, and then in a handy-dandy minute, she was gone. Allie did not know if she should laugh or cry.

All she could do was close her eyes and wait for the handy-dandy pills to make her feel fine and dandy.

CHAPTER 41

A Colorless Liquid

Back in his hotel room, the Mexican gingerly put the vial on the table beside the container that was to hold ice but was now filled with dirt. He had purchased a small bag of potting soil from the nearest dollar store, and he planned to pour some of the vial into the dirt to see exactly what would happen. He knew he should turn the vial over to his handlers; however, he had learned that it was best to be absolutely sure that what you were handing over was exactly what they wanted, and he needed to see how it worked.

And being the crook that he was, he had toyed with the idea of taking some of the content of the vial for himself. He would turn the vial over to the cartel and receive his considerable reward money. Then he would take the vial content he had taken for himself to a lab in Mexico. Once they determined the chemical makeup, he could reproduce it himself. He would build a laboratory and sell his product to countries of the world and become a millionaire. No, a billionaire. He felt dizzy with the thought of the money that would pour into his company.

His hand was shaking with excitement, and so he poured some whiskey into a glass and tilted it to let the harsh liquid pour down his throat to steady his nerves. He flinched as it burned his throat on the way down, and his imagination moved to a time when he would have so much money from the sale of his vial product that he could buy the finest liquor that was so smooth it would not burn when swallowed.

He pried the top of the vial off, being careful not to bend it, and then he slowly lifted the small cork from the vial. The liquid was almost colorless, but when you held it up to the light, a soft-blue sheen seemed to emit from it. He slowly tipped it on its side and held it over the pot of dirt. He found he had to quash the thought of keeping it all for himself. He could tell the cartel that he had not been able to get the vial from the girl, but they would know, and they would kill him in a heartbeat.

First, he had to test the liquid in the vial to be sure it worked, and so he allowed six drops of the liquid to disappear into the dirt before he jammed the cork back into the neck of the vial. He suddenly realized that he had been holding his breath, and he took in several huge gulps of air to satisfy his screaming lungs. He was not cut out for this kind of work. He immensely enjoyed using the stiletto blade of his father's time, but this was where he was in real time. He deftly replaced the cork and the top and softly placed the vial back onto the table.

He stared at the pot of dirt. Now what? Should he add water? Should he put it by the window to get more light? Should he just do nothing? He decided on doing nothing. He looked around the room and found the TV remote and pointed it at the television. The picture immediately flashed on, and he dialed to the news channel. After a few commercials, the talking head was reporting on a possible mugging attempt at the local airport where a man and a woman had been attacked, and both were taken to the hospital with minor injuries.

The airport authorities were reminding people to be vigilant when traveling even though an airport was reportedly one of the safest places for tourists and this mugging was reported as a rarity. The Mexican laughed. A rarity indeed! This mugging had resulted in a rare opportunity for him. He laughed loudly as he swallowed the last of the whiskey. First, he would sleep, and then he would test the liquid in the vial to see what the contents would do when introduced to dirt. Only then would he return to Mexico and turn the vial over to his Mexican cartel handlers.

He was patient, and he would wait until he knew the secret of the vial.

CHAPTER 42

A Look of Bookends

The father and the son desperately needed to talk, and both agreed that they were not comfortable talking indoors. It was hard to think that bugging devices may have been placed inside their homes and their cars, but they were both scared, and so they agreed to take a walk in the park. The fall weather was not being kind, and the wind whipped around every corner. So they bundled up and set off toward the park. They were not very tall, and each wore several sweaters under a large overcoat, and side by side they looked like bookends. The Third talked, and The Second listened.

It turned out to be cathartic for the son as he meticulously outlined every move and thought he had over the last months leading up to and including his inability to reach his friend, Lenny. His recitation of all these facts slowly jelled into a chilling picture, and when he had finished, both men stopped walking.

The Third braced for his father to berate him and raise his voice as was his custom, but The Second only stood in silence. Finally, he looked at his son, and with tears coursing down his cheeks, he said, "Son, I am so proud of you." This proved to be too much for The Third as he was prepared for parental anger and not parental praise, and he, too, gave in to tears. The two men leaned against each other in the cold air, each feeling the warmth of shared emotions that was so rare for a father and a son of their generation.

*****

Blake had been examined by the emergency room staff at the hospital, and while his injuries were not serious, consisting of bumps and bruises, it was decided to admit him for a twenty-four-hour period. He had vigorously objected, but it fell on deaf ears.

Allie was unconscious and required immediate care and observation and was taken to a separate floor. Blake found himself trapped in the hospital system, and because he and Allie were not related, he was not allowed to visit her. He was frantic because he knew that she was in danger and alone. The policy of the hospital staff was set in stone, and Blake found that no amount of pleading or demanding would get him information about Allie. Finally, he was able to bribe a young college student whose job it was to push patients in wheelchairs who were being released from the hospital and escort them to their cars.

Blake did not know that Allie no longer had the vial around her neck, and he was certain she would need protection. The man who had attacked her in the airport and who had knocked Blake out had succeeded in disappearing into the airport crowd. Blake was certain he would return to follow Allie, and so she was, in Blake's mind, still in danger.

Once he was released from the hospital, Blake immediately requested that his intelligence contact in the government arrange that Allie be placed in a private room and given twenty-four-hour protection. The hospital had to comply with this arrangement; however, they still would not allow him visitation rights. He could not visit Allie in her protected hospital room, and he was under no illusions that whoever had attacked her would return and continue to stalk her. Blake had parked his car where he could observe the entrance to the hospital lobby and where he could also see the windows to the room Allie was in on the second floor. It was a catch-22, and all he could do was hope that his presence and the military protection at her hospital room were enough to prevent the man from getting to Allie before he could.

Blake rightly felt as if he was in limbo.

CHAPTER 43

Burnout

Jim sat at his desk, and for the first time in many years, he wanted to throw something and yell as loud as he could in anger and frustration. Instead, he grabbed some paperwork that was to go into the trash, and he furiously ripped it up into several pieces. It did not change his mood, but the action did help.

Oh, where on earth are you, Allie? he thought. Jim had not realized exactly how much work Allie did in preparing the weekly and monthly activity schedules for Whispering Palms. On top of all that preparation, she also managed the day-to-day personal management and dealing with all the in-house residents. Jim had not hired an assistant activities director because Allie had taken the position of activities director and seamlessly made it seem as if all the work and activities "just happened." He made a mental note to himself that as soon as Allie returned, he would hire someone to help her. Working seven days a week for over eight hours a day would soon cause burnout for any employee, and Jim did not want that to happen, if indeed, it had not happened already.

Jim felt a wave of guilt wash over him as he suddenly wondered if her disappearance was connected to a physical and mental burnout related to her work. Wouldn't he have seen that in her? She always seemed so in control of herself. In fact, he had been amazed at how she always had a ready smile for everyone. Perhaps making the change from the Gardens to Whispering Palms had been too much for her without an assistant. He shook his head and silently chided himself for not being more observant of his new employee. His memory pulled up conversations he had had with Allie, and he could not find anything she had done or said that would indicate undue stress. But then he knew that employees often withheld their true feelings from their bosses. He had done it himself in the early years. Still, in her personal presentations or her paperwork that he now had access to and her associations with the residents, none of them showed undue stress.

He had kept in touch with the Missing Persons Department at the police department as well as Ms. Wilheim, Allie's neighbor; and of course, the employees at Whispering Palms all knew to contact him the minute they had any news. Jim had to admit he had never expected her absence to be longer than a day or two, and he stopped shuffling papers and slumped back into his chair and hung his head. He surprised himself when he felt a few tears slip down his cheeks. His anger gave way to fear and sadness as he realized he was on the verge of thinking she may never come back. He sat very still, allowing the emotion to wash over him, and his mind spoke volumes. *Allie. Please, please do not let anything happen to yourself. You are too good a person to just disappear. Come back. We all need you here.*

Jim shook his head to clear his thinking and then set his mind toward the paperwork in front of him. In the meantime, he was juggling the activities she had already set up as well as all the demanding needs of his job as director.

He knew he could not keep up this pace for too much longer.

CHAPTER 44

More Handy-Dandy

Once the handy-dandy pain pills kicked in from the handy-dandy nurse, Allie found she could slowly drag herself up to a sitting position. She took several deep breaths as she allowed her mind to clear. She decided to think back to the first day she began her new job at Whispering Palms, and she sat in her beloved red car in the parking lot and prepared to begin her new job.

She meticulously went over all the events that had transpired, and she was inwardly amazed and even a little proud of all she had accomplished. When she came to the part about her friendship with The Third, she could not stop a smile from erupting deep within as she realized how much she treasured their friendship. And when she thought about Blake, her heart skipped a few beats. She realized he was one of the last thoughts she had because her thoughts reached the part where someone had dragged her down onto the airport terminal floor. In her memory, she saw Blake's body as it moved through the air to tackle someone, and then her thoughts and memory abruptly stopped.

"Oh no! Where is Blake?" and she startled herself when she realized she had spoken these words out loud. They had both been attacked at the airport, and she was in a private hospital room, but where was Blake? And where was the vial that she realized was no longer on a chain around her neck? She reached for the button to summon the nurse, and without intending to, she pushed it again and again and again because she wanted answers now.

The handy-dandy nurse came bustling in, carrying a tray of medications, and immediately came to Allie's bedside. "Good heavens, girl! You would think the hospital was on fire! You only need to push the call button once, you know. We are all very busy, but we come as soon as we can." She took the button from Allie's hand and patted her arm as she put the tray down on Allie's bed. As was apparently her nurse's bedside manner, she did not wait to hear what Allie had wanted, and she continued talking.

"I see you are sitting up, so those handy-dandy pain pills are doing their job. I have some more here, and I will get you some water, and you can take them after you have your meal. Then, once I finish my rounds, I will come back, and we can fill in your admission paperwork because you were not fine and dandy when you came in here and then..."

It was at this point that Allie loudly interrupted her. She knew this handy-dandy nurse would just continue with her nonstop handy-dandy talking, and so Allie dug deep into the remaining strength that she had and said, "Oh, for heaven's sake, stop talking! Please! Just stop talking!" And she startled the nurse so much that she did just that. She stopped talking and stared silently at Allie.

"Thank you," Allie said. "I'm sorry to be yelling, but I need to ask some questions." Allie continued to speak so the nurse could not. "Where are my things? The things I had when they brought me here? My purse? My carry-on bag. And I had a chain around my neck, and it is gone. And I was brought in here with another person, and where is he? And..."

The nurse had recovered her momentum by this time, and she put up her hand in front of Allie's face to break the stream of words and said, "It is all right. It is all right, Allie. All your valuables are in a hospital bag and stored in the hospital vault in human resources. The man who was brought in with you has been discharged, and I can..."

Allie was not usually so insistent, but she rudely interrupted her again and said, "Well, I need to contact him immediately, and I want to have all my personal effects here with me. And I want to know when I can leave and…"

This time it was the handy-dandy nurse's turn to interrupt, and she said, "Of course, Allie. You can have all those things as soon as we have you feeling fine and dandy and…"

This time Allie literally screamed, "I do not care about feeling fine and dandy. In fact, I do not want to hear about anything that's fine and dandy or handy-dandy. I want my things. And I want to leave. Now!" The force and sound of her own voice startled Allie as well as the handy-dandy nurse, and the two ladies stared at each other in a deafening silence. The nurse quietly spoke. "I'll get your doctor to come and see you." And she picked up the medication tray and was gone before Allie realized she had apparently won the yelling match. Suddenly, tears erupted and splashed over her cheeks.

Allie slumped back onto the pillows and gave herself permission to cry.

CHAPTER 45

Drastic Measures

The Second and The Third had found a bench in the park, and they settled onto it, huddling together against the wind. Neither spoke. The Second was frantically thinking, and The Third was just feeling frantic, waiting to see what his father would do. Finally, The Second spoke.

"Son," he said, "this situation calls for drastic measures." The Third thought to himself, *Good lord! I knew that*, but instead, he decided to go along with the statement and let his father feel as if he was in control.

"We need a plane," The Second said. "We need to get a chartered plane to take us up to Kensington where your friend Lenny lives. You said you sent the girl, with the vial, to deliver it to Lenny, but now you cannot reach Lenny. Nor can you reach the girl. And they may both be in danger, so we need a plane." He took out his phone and began punching in numbers while he continued to speak.

"I have…well, let us just call them excellent connections, as I know people who own and can fly airplanes. And I have money. Lots of it. Not that you would know as you always had your head in a test tube, so to speak. I always knew that you viewed money as an annoyance, and so I was able to cushion your lifestyle so that you would not have to worry about the ever-loving dollar." The Second chuckled to himself. "And you did not. You just put your head down, and over the years, your experiments became the center of your life.

With so many failures, I thought you would eventually give up. But you did not. You and Lenny just kept plugging away. And now, we must go and find out why you cannot reach Lenny. And we must intercept that girl that you sent to find him. And to do all that, we need a plane."

Apparently, someone came on the other end of the phone, and The Second said, "Hello. Freedman Carver the Second here. To whom am I speaking? Kevin? Yes, Kevin. I need to get a reliable pilot with a small aircraft. Right. Immediately, if not sooner." He softly chuckled at his own little joke on words. "Yes, right away, and money is no object. I will pay whatever the going rate is with a generous bonus thrown in if we do not have to wait. Yes, tomorrow morning is perfect. I will make all the arrangements at the local airfield and forward them on to you. Wonderful. We will expect to meet the aircraft at seven in the morning. Yes, thank you. Oh, and is Jeremy still overseeing all the arrangements for your airline? He is. Please give him my best regards, and I will be in touch with him once we are in the air. Yes. Thank you. Goodbye."

The Second sat very still, staring off into space, and The Third found himself unable to say anything, being totally amazed at the control and poise his father had exhibited. Finally, the father turned and looked at his son and said, "And that, my son, is how you get an airplane when you need one. Now we need to get home, throw a few clothes into a suitcase, and get some sleep because 7:00 AM will be here before we know it. Let us go." He stood and began walking away.

The Third had to gather himself together to run after The Second as his father strode into the wind.

CHAPTER 46

Between a Rock and a Hard Place

The sun rose on a chilly fall day, and a soft haze blanketed the cool air, giving the impression that a gray blanket had spread itself over the area. There was no doubt that winter air was just around the corner, and the fall sun tried valiantly to give the impression that it could warm the air if given a chance.

It was too early for most humans to be up and about. Allie was still asleep in her cozy hospital bed. Blake had staked out a spot in the hospital parking lot, and he held a cup of scalding coffee close to his body to feel the warmth of it through the cardboard cup. Not being allowed to visit Allie, he could only hover in place and hope to be there when she was released from the hospital.

In Seattle, The Second and The Third were in a taxi, riding toward the small airfield on the outskirts of the main airport. Neither had slept much. They sat in the back seat, not talking and each struggling to stay awake as the warmth of the taxi and the slight swaying motion threatened to put them to sleep. Each man found a little comfort thinking that once they were inside their newly chartered airplane, they could doze off. Neither man realized that flying in a small airplane was not conducive to sleeping. They would learn.

*****

As the darkness of night slowly gave way to the brightness of day, the Mexican had gone to the bathroom, and on his way back to bed, he looked at the pot of soil sitting in the middle of his hotel room. Nothing. No spurts of green growth. Just dirt. He wondered if it needed more water. He had already watered it. He had put it in the bathroom underneath the overhead heating lamp for warmth. Nothing seemed to work. He had carefully allowed six drops of the liquid from the vial to disappear into the dirt, and he expected… what? Something? Anything. Growth!

He was beginning to worry about turning the vial over to the cartel handlers. They would experience the same lack of growth, and they would suspect he had switched the liquid. And they would find and kill him in a heartbeat. He was between a rock and a hard place. Damned if he did and damned if he did not. He poured himself another stiff drink. Not a brilliant idea at seven in the morning, but he was desperate. This Mexican was not the brightest bulb on the bush. He had the liquid from the vial. He had dirt and water and heat from a lamp.

His greedy mind and his limited intelligence only knew that the liquid in the vial did not work. Why had that happened? So why didn't it work? He was angry and frustrated and really getting scared. The cartel knew he was the only one in possession of the vial, and they would think that he must have substituted the liquid. He was a dead man. He poured another drink. And then another. His thinking became fuzzy, but his fear subsided with the increase of liquor in his body. He needed time. He need time to think. So far, he was safe. He had not told the cartel which hotel he was in, and he had checked in under an alias. So he was safe. For now. He glared at the pot of dirt. It had only been twenty-four hours. Maybe it needed another day. He decided that was it. He would hunker down in this obscure hotel room and wait for the dirt to erupt in growth. In the meantime, he had plenty of liquor, and every hotel had room service, so he could wait it out. It was the pot of dirt and himself.

He took another drink. The warmth of it told him that he had made the best decision. He would wait. He had the vial in his possession, and it would eventually make him a million…no…it would make him a billionaire. Life was good, and so he waited.

And he drank and imagined that life would be good.

CHAPTER 47

A Bad Movie Plot

Allie awoke with a start. She had been dreaming that she was running from behind one pole to the next pole in a forest of poles. It was a frightening thought in the dream and an even worse thought when she was awake. She decided she was not going to stay one more hour in the hospital. She picked up the phone, and reading the phone directory, she called the human resources office. When a female voice came on the phone, she took a deep breath and gave her best performance of a very frustrated and busy nurse.

"This is the nurse calling from the second floor, and I am too busy to come down and get the valuables for, oh, let us see—what is her name? Alice. Angie. No wait. I remember now. It's Allie. Allie Birks, and she is such a disagreeable patient. All she does is complain. Anyway, send her belongings to room, ah yes, to room 216. Thank heavens, her doctor is discharging her, and I am short-staffed up here, or I would come down myself. Thanks. Room 216. Stat."

Allie slammed down the phone in a supposed impatience and had to stifle a laugh. "Allie Birks is such a disagreeable patient," she repeated to herself. She knew she had to find a way to send word to Blake, so she got up from the bed and looked around the room. Her clothing hung in a closet behind her bed, and she pulled it off the hanger and quickly dressed. She took the chart that was hanging at side of the bed, pulled off a sheet of paper, and wrote in large letters Meet me with an arrow pointing down. If Blake was outside of the hospital, he might be watching her window, and she needed to let him see her. She went to the window and held up the sign. *Good lord,* she thought, *this is beginning to be like the plot in a bad movie.*

Blake was leaning against his rental car fighting fatigue and straining to keep his eyes open. Suddenly, he saw some movement in the second-floor window, and there was Allie holding up a sign that read "Meet me." *Attagirl,* he thought. *We need to work together*, and this time he was very aware of a warm flush that ran through his body when he saw her. He shook his head and thought, *Oh, Allie. You are getting to me, aren't you?*

His job had very strict protocols against becoming involved with a client, but emotions do not pay attention to rules. The Intelligence Bureau of the United States would pull him from his assignment immediately if they suspected he might be compromising the situation. He stood still, silently willing himself to view Allie as just another person. He was proud of his ability to control his emotions, and he was determined this situation would be no different.

Allie could not see if Blake was able to see her sign from the hospital window, but she had to do something, so she took a chance. She instinctively felt that Blake was a new friend, and she might not be in this part of the journey alone.

Allie now realized she might be in danger, and she was a long way from the safety of Whispering Palms. She had thought this trip would be nothing more than a quick flight to take the vial up to Mr. Freedman's friend Lenny's laboratory. She never envisioned it would be anything more.

Suddenly, a hospital employee burst into the room clutching a bag that contained Allie's personal belongings. She frantically looked around, and then, in an obvious state of confusion, she stood perfectly still and dropped the bag onto the hospital bed. Allie sensed she needed to do something before this person could have second thoughts and take her belongings back to human resources, and so she said, "Ah, those are the personal belongings for room 216. Good. Thank you for bringing them up so promptly. Good work."

The employee did not move, and she kept frantically looking around the room, and so Allie said, "Oh yes, that is right, I must sign for them. Give me the slip, and I will take this off your hands and you can get back to your desk at your office." Allie reached out and took the slip from the employee's hand, and getting a pen from the bedside table, she scribbled something unreadable on it and shoved it into the girl's hand at the same time taking her elbow and moving her toward the door. The employee stopped, and the two females silently stared into the other's eyes. It was only for a few moments, but Allie felt as if it was a lifetime. Finally, the employee broke her staring trance and said, "Yes. I do need to get back to the office." She paused and then said, "They didn't want me to get the belongings for room 216, but I felt that poor, frantic nurse was waiting, and I didn't think we should let her down."

Allie nodded, patting the employee on the arm and said, "You did the right thing. The nurse is delivering medications to the other rooms right now, but when she gets back, I will tell her what you said. Thank you."

The employee was obviously grateful to hear that praise, but she seemed to be rooted in place, so Allie gently took her elbow and moved her toward the door. "I wish we had more employees like you, and I know you need to get back to your office. I will take over from here." The employee straightened up, and as she moved toward the door, Allie added, "Just one thing. It would be best if you kept this transaction quiet for a while. You know how touchy they are and…" Allie faltered, searching for more words when the employee spoke in a bubbly tone. "Oh my, I certainly know how touchy 'they' can be! You have my word. I will keep this quiet, and no one will know before they need to."

Allie felt as if she had won the lottery, but she calmly said "thank you," and then the employee was gone, and Allie moved toward the bed to sit down. Suddenly, she felt as if all her breath had escaped from her body.

Good lord, she thought, *what just happened?*

CHAPTER 48

Rocky Road

The two men were so tightly wedged into the seats of the small Cessna that neither could move or turn or even take a deep breath. The noise was deafening, and as the tiny plane rolled down the uneven runway, the pilot yelled some instructions at them, but they could not hear nor move and so as one, they held their breath and clutched onto each other. The Third was so scared he finally decided if he was going to die, he might as well be present for it, and he managed to turn his head and yell into his father's ear, "We need…" and The Second decided to finish his sentence, and he yelled back, "A bigger plane." It was as if both men could see those words floating in a big bubble in the plane. And it was funny. Those words—"We need a bigger plane" would become their words to say to each other in the future whenever they felt they were heading for trouble.

*****

Allie realized that she could not take the chance of another employee coming into the room, so she picked up her bag, went behind the tall screen beside the hospital bed, and began to change to warmer clothes to leave the hospital. She was almost dressed when she thought she heard a sound in the room, and she froze. Suddenly, a voice said, "Is someone in here?" Allie fought to keep herself calm and quiet, and she held her breath as the voice apparently called out to another person.

"Helen. I thought they said there was a lady in room 216, but there is no one here."

Another voice said, "I do not have the room number. You will have to go back to human resources to check it out."

The first voice said with obvious annoyance, "Oh, drat! I am so far behind now. I will just do it on my way back."

The second voice said, "Whatever! But be sure to close the door so another nurse does not wander in on her shift."

Allie closed her eyes and listened, and finally, after what seemed like an eternity, she heard a soft whoosh. It was the soft rubber that was attached to the bottom of the door, and then, when the door reached its frame, there was a soft click, and the door closed. Allie seemed to be frozen in place, and suddenly, she realized she could not move. She needed to breathe, so she soundlessly allowed herself to exhale, and only then could she gently feel that she could control the movement of her body.

Meanwhile, Blake had entered the hospital at the emergency room entrance and quietly moved down the hallway until he reached the lobby. There were quite a few people milling about, and he gravitated to a spot where he could appear to be reading his newspaper while waiting to meet someone. Most hospital lobbies were the central point from which the halls branched out to the different hospital sections, and he hoped this one was no different. It seemed he had barely lifted his newspaper when he spotted Allie moving from a hallway into the lobby.

Making a split decision, he lowered his newspaper and moved toward her and reached out to take her arm. He laughed out loud as he said, "I know that most people are anxious to be discharged from a hospital, but you're trying to break speed limits." Allie looked as if she was about to speak and Blake continued. "I know I'm usually on time in picking you up, but I had a wicked job in finding a parking space, so you can slow down now and catch your breath."

Allie stopped and looked at him, and out of surprise, she started to laugh. Blake took her arm, and smoothly moving her toward the exit, he said, "And I'm so glad that you're in a good mood because I see that there's a little ice cream parlor in the center of the lobby, and they have all kinds of unusual flavors."

By this time Allie had regained most of her composure, and falling into the conversation, she said, "Oh, that's so good because I could certainly use an ice cream cone, and there's a perfect flavor that fits our situation."

Blake said, "Well, I have looked at their flavors, and I think the flavor that fits our situation might be, let me see. I will guess twisted lemon. Our paths got twisted, and it seems this trip is turning out to be a lemon."

Allie laughed and said, "Oh wow, that's so good but no. I was thinking of rocky road because our trip turned out to be a…" And together they said "rocky road."

Allie laughed again, and Blake thought he had never heard such a delightful, engaging laugh. It kind of bubbled out into the air. His subconscious warned him about getting emotionally involved, but his present "thinking mind" told his subconscious mind to shut up. He gently guided her toward a bench and said, "You sit here, and I will get us two rocky road cones. I will be right back."

Allie did as she was told and slowly lowered herself onto the bench as she watched Blake hustle over to get their ice cream cones, and she thought to herself, *What a delightful man. It is so easy to be with him.* Then she chided herself and thought, *That is enough, Allie. This trip was to complete the vial's journey for Mr. Carver and not to enjoy the presence of a good-looking man. However, Mr. Carver did warn me that I may run into a little…how did he put it? Traffic.* She touched her neck where the bruises were and flinched at the soreness. Blake had almost stopped the man who attacked her, and she wondered where the vial was now."

*****

The vial seemed to be mocking the man as he looked at it lying on the bedside table. There had been absolutely no sign of growth in the dirt he had put in the hotel ice cube container. He angrily took another drink of liquor. He no longer poured it into a glass and was now drinking directly from the bottle. He had a little trouble focusing his eyes, but he could see that there was no growth, and he spoke out loud saying almost every swear word he knew.

He almost wished that he had just handed the vial over to the Mexican cartel and not decided to test the vial's liquid. Then they would be the ones to test it and find out that it was a dud, but he knew they would think he had somehow changed the liquid in the vial, and he would be dead in the water. His liquor-fogged mind wondered why we say "dead in the water" to describe when things are not going well. He kept repeating the phrase to himself, "Dead in the water. Dead in the water."

If he had paid attention in his history class in high school, he would have realized that long ago, sailors had coined that saying. When wind was the power that drove their boats, and there was no wind, and the boats just sat without moving, the sailors called their situation as being dead in the water. Going nowhere. And the plan of the Mexican was doing just that. Going nowhere. Dead in the water.

He took another drink and glared at the dirt.

CHAPTER 49

Stranger Things Might Happen

Allie opened her purse to get her mirror to check her hair and makeup, and her eyes fell on a vial snuggled safely in the pouch of her makeup kit, and she smiled to herself. *Mr. Carver III was so right,* she thought. He had given her two vials. One to wear around her neck and one to carry in her purse. His reasoning was that, as she passed through Canada, it might be that customs and immigration might decide to confiscate the vial around her neck, and so she should carry a second vial in her purse. At the time Allie thought that he was being overly cautious, but she humored him, and it turned out he was right that she would need a second vial.

It was a good thing that Allie did not know how many people were following her because of the vial. The Mexican cartel had sent three men, each working independently of the other, and because they had not heard from any of them, they had dispatched two more men, and this time the men knew each other. They were, in fact, two of the Mexicans' elite force and worked together so well that it was almost as if they had the same brain. Once they had received their orders, they rarely had to speak; they were so in tune with their objective. So it was that there were the two of them and Blake, who was working for the Americans, following the vial, and then there were the two scientists who were stuffed in a small Cessna. And Allie was totally unaware of it all. She had promised The Third that she would deliver the vial to his friend, Lenny, and while her stint in the hospital had interrupted her northward trip, she was still going to do just that.

Meanwhile, Lenny was still battling his amnesia. He had missed answering the phone, and then he had uncharacteristically dissolved in tears of frustration and fear. He had stopped crying and had the feeling that humans have when they are unequivocally and emotionally spent. He was exhausted and had no desire to move.

He did not know if he had been sitting still for one minute or one hour, but then he heard and then felt the rumbling of his stomach. And he remembered hunger. In fact, he was so hungry he was almost sick to his stomach. He had found the kitchen, and there was a loaf of white bread, and in the white box he found strawberry jam, and in a cupboard a huge, almost full jar of peanut butter. It was probably a throw-back memory from his youth, but he knew how to make a peanut-butter-and-jam sandwich. He was not neat in the sandwich making, and with the jam literally flowing out of the sandwich, he inhaled it. Of course, it was not enough, but by the middle of the third sandwich, he realized he could stop stuffing himself. And there was milk. Wonderful, cold milk, and finally he stopped and took a deep breath and found his stomach no longer complained of hunger. He had failed to answer the ringing phone, but he had succeeded in feeding himself. He felt a small chuckle bubble up out of his chest, and then he made an actual laugh and then another, and soon he gave in to hysterical laughter. It was a marvelous relief, and he sat back and let the emotion wash over his body. He decided life was good.

When he calmed down, he thought, *I do not know my name or what I do for a living, but at least my stomach has given up on complaining for the moment.* He suddenly realized his headache was gone too, and his thinking was clearer. Then the same picture of The Third appeared in his mind. This time he had control of his thoughts. He carefully studied the picture in his mind. "Okay, maybe he is my father? Nope. Not old enough. Must be a good friend. And maybe he was the one who was calling on the phone. Wait! Maybe there is a way that my phone can tell me who was calling." He picked up the receiver of the landline, and it had a bank of numbers and buttons that said "Talk" and "Off" and arrows going every which way. Apparently, it was a Panasonic brand, and it also had a small window that gave the time of day and the date. There was a small sign that said "MENU" and another that said "MUTE." He saw "CID" and "REDIAL" and "SP Phone," and "FLASH/CALL WAIT." The more he studied it, the more he could feel his head beginning to ache. He held it up to his ear and no one was there, and all he heard was a long, single sound. He felt deflated because this was not helping, and so all he could do was wait for the phone to ring again, and this time, he would have it close enough to answer.

He felt and heard a long sound that was a sigh coming from his chest. So taking stock, he knew he was safe. He was apparently in his own home. He could feed himself, and it seemed someone had tried to reach him, and they would try again. This time he would be ready to answer the ringing. He could feel the throbbing in his head beginning to rise again, so he stopped projecting thoughts within his head. He moved toward the couch where there was a big blanket. He did not know it was called a quilt and had been made for him by his mother, but he knew it felt warm and protecting. He poured himself a huge glass of water, and keeping the phone beside him, he sank onto the couch and prepared himself to answer the phone the next time it rang.

And so, Lenny waited.

CHAPTER 50

Flight 1062

Allie had told The Third that she would call his friend, Lenny, once she reached the Kensington airport. The Third had told her a little of his and Lenny's history and their lifelong friendship. He said she was to expect to see a man who was in the age range of The Third and that Lenny had never married nor been around women, so he would appear as being either shy, or he would act almost as if she did not exist. Allie was not to take it personally. It was just Lenny's way.

Once Allie met Blake in the hospital lobby, she knew she had experienced a setback having been attacked in the airport, but now she felt as if she would complete her mission. So she decided to call Lenny and fill him in on what had happened to her. While she and Blake had established a tremendous sense of comradeship over the time of their flights, neither had told the other about their true reasons for traveling—Allie to deliver the vial and Blake to keep Allie and the vial in his sights. Blake, hoping to have Allie give the United States the rights to the contents of the vial, and Allie with the sole purpose of delivering the vial to The Third's friend, Lenny.

Allie now understood that it was best for the vial and the chemical makeup to be safely stored in The Third's laboratory that was in Lenny's home, and so she had looked forward to meeting this Lenny and handing over the vial. Allie then planned to stay a couple of days and sightsee whatever there was to sightsee near the Arctic Circle. She was already feeling a homesickness type of ache as she thought of her home, her beloved Oreo, and Mrs. Wilheim. Long-distance traveling was fine, but it did not take long for travelers to long to be in familiar surroundings and sleeping in their own beds. Allie was grateful that she had the health and strength to make this long trip; however, she was glad that she was on the last leg. And with this in mind, she looked up the phone number that The Third had given her, and she dialed Lenny's home phone.

*****

He must have been dreaming. Lenny did not know how long he had been sitting on the couch, and in truth, he probably had dozed off, and so he was not sure why he suddenly found himself sitting upright on the couch. He frantically looked around the room, giving himself the feeling of being dizzy. But within a few seconds his mind clicked in, and he remembered. He did not remember his name or where he was, but he remembered enough to calm himself down.

Then he heard it again. The phone had slipped beneath the quilt, and it was ringing again. His hand moved to the sound, and he threw back the quilt, and then the ringing sounded deafening to him, so much so that he momentarily froze in place and stared at it. He knew he wanted to pick it up, but a blanket of fear had overtaken him. He now knew he did not know who he was, and so how would he know who was calling? It rang two more times before he finally snapped out of his paralysis and reached for the receiver.

Lenny clutched the phone and tried to speak, but his throat felt as if someone was strangling him, and when he spoke, only a soft sigh of air came out with no sound. Allie was on the other end of the line listening to the phone ringing when suddenly the ringing stopped, but no one spoke. Allie hesitated, but then habit clicked in, and she said, "Hello. Hello? Is this Lenny?"

Lenny's habit also took over, and he cleared his throat, and instead of saying "hello," he brusquely said, "Who is this?" Allie immediately brightened at hearing Lenny's voice, and she said, "Hello. This is Allie calling." And she waited for a reply.

Lenny was fighting two conflicting emotions as he fought fear because of his amnesia, but also a joy that felt like it was a huge erupting waterspout of happiness in hearing someone's voice. He gripped the phone tighter and said, "Allie. Yes, Allie."

On the other end of the phone, Allie was reminding herself of The Third's words. Lenny had never married nor been around women, so he would appear shy, or he might act as if she did not exist and not to take it personally, so she brightly pressed on. "Yes. Hi, Lenny. I wanted to let you know that I had a little setback in my trip, but everything is fine now, and I am in the airport in Seattle and about to get on the next flight to Kensington."

Lenny was trying desperately to follow her quickly moving comments, so he grasped on the last words he heard. "The next flight to Kensington?" By now Allie was in full swing in her part of the conversation, and she cheerily kept talking. "Yes. The plane will leave in about thirty minutes, and the flight number is 1062, and I will be wearing a red jacket, so you will know who to look for when you pick me up."

Lenny had grabbed a pencil and was frantically scribbling on a notepad by the telephone, and he repeated, "Flight number 1062. A red jacket."

Allie was convinced this voice on the other end belonged to The Third's friend Lenny, and she chattered on. "Yes. I look forward to meeting you, Lenny. Bye now." And she quickly hung up as she wanted to get to the gate so she would not miss her flight.

Lenny stood holding the phone receiver, which now had the same long sound of the dial tone emanating from it. Slowly, as if in an exaggerated slow-motion move, he gingerly put the phone back on its hook, and he stared at what he had written.

Allie. Kensington. Flt. 1062. Red jacket. Lenny.

CHAPTER 51

Let Me Help You

The tires squealed loudly as the small Cessna slammed into the runway, and the plane took several bounces before the landing gear grabbed hold of the rough tarmac and gravity and the pilot could straighten out the landing. They had finally arrived at Kensington airport, and both men silently vowed never to ever fly in a small plane again. Their young pilot yelled back at them as they rolled up to one of the hangars that sat just off the main runway. Neither man moved, nor could they hear or understand what he was saying when finally, gratefully, the single-engine plane's motor stopped, and the quiet was indeed deafening in its silence.

The Third clenched his stomach muscles so he would not be sick to his stomach, and The Second was frantically pulling at the clasp of his seat belt, trying to eject himself from the airplane seat. The young pilot had easily climbed down from the plane, and seeing that The Second was struggling, he moved toward him and said, "Here. Let me get that for you." Normally, The Second would have waved him off because he hated it when young people would offer to help him. But this time he understood he could not undo the buckle, so he said, "Thank you." The pilot reached over and undid The Third's seat belt as well, and almost as one, both men kind of stumbled and fell forward out of the seats, and the pilot put out his arms and helped them both to stand up. Neither spoke, and so the pilot filled the conversation void and said, "I hope you enjoyed the flight. Sorry about the run of turbulence back there, but it is the time of the year for that."

By this time The Second had somewhat regained his equilibrium and he gruffly said, "No. I mean, yes. It was all fine." Feeling more confident having been able to hear his own voice, he continued. "We need to rent a car."

The pilot immediately went into his "I can help you" mode and said, "Yes. Of course. If you will follow me, I will take you to that section of the terminal, and we can pick up your luggage on the way there." And he turned and quickly moved off. The two elderly men scrambled to get their land legs back as they uneasily moved off in the direction that the young man had gone.

The Second realized that this young man had safely flown them to their destination and was still helping them, so he fumbled for his wallet to have a tip ready when they would arrive at the car rental station with their luggage. The Third would not have ever known to tip someone, and he was busily trying to tie both his shoes, which had apparently become undone during the flight. They looked like a father taking control of a situation and a son who was just along for the ride and did not have to take any responsibility for their situation.

When they had been safely reunited with their luggage and the pilot had been given a substantial tip, The Second told The Third to use the restroom to freshen up, and he took out a slip of paper from his wallet and proceeded to punch the numbers on his cell phone that would connect his call to Lenny."

He calmly listened to the phone ring waiting for him, waiting for Lenny, to answer his phone.

CHAPTER 52

The Couch and the Quilt

Having successfully made it through the phone conversation with Allie, Lenny was filled with the euphoria of confidence and turned into a little fireball of energy. "Oh! Oh! Lenny," he said out loud. My name is Lenny. I am Lenny." And Allie knows me, and she is at an airport and…" Suddenly, he came to the end of the energetic spurt, and he more quietly repeated, "Lenny. I am Lenny."

He stood listening to his breath, too overwhelmed to say anything more, when suddenly the phone receiver he was holding began to ring, scaring him so much that he dropped the phone. He immediately said the swear words that he had not forgotten. Suddenly afraid that the ringing might stop as it did before, he literally dove down to the floor, scrambling to pick up the phone, and when he finally got it to his ear, he blurted out, "Yes, yes, I am here. Do not hang up, I am here!"

On the other end of the phone, listening to "Do not hang up. I am here!" The Second could not help himself, and he burst out laughing, saying, "Yes, I know you are there. And I am here too. And who is speaking please?" He knew it was Lenny, but he still asked who was speaking.

It was almost more than Lenny could handle. His universe had gone from him not knowing who he was or where he was to being able to successfully talk to two different people in two different phone calls. He closed his eyes and mentally drew upon inner strength so that he could project a normal tone of voice.

"Hello again. This is Lenny, and I apologize for my comments as I have had problems with my phone, and I did not want to lose contact with—with whoever is calling me, so I would appreciate it if you would identify yourself. Please."

The Second said, "Hello, Lenny. I am the father of your friend, Freedman Carver the Third. We have just arrived in Kensington, and we are at the car rental booth at the airport.

Lenny did not say anything as he found it was hard to keep up with fast-moving conversations. The Second waited for Lenny to speak, and when he heard nothing, he thought that he might have lost the telephone connection. "Hello, hello, Lenny? Oh, drat, I have lost contact with him. It must be the Wi-Fi signal up here," and he hung up, leaving Lenny holding the phone, still trying to find his voice to speak. His headache had returned. The voice on the phone had said he had a friend whose name was Freedman Carver III. He had a friend.

Lenny suddenly realized his energy level felt as if it was down to zero. His head hurt. His body hurt. His mind hurt. He desperately needed to rest. If he slept, he knew he would feel better. The couch and the quilt seemed to reach out to him, and he did not want to think anymore. He wanted to sleep. So he curled up on the couch in a fetal position and wrapped the quilt around his body, and within a minute, Lenny was sound asleep.

Allie was at the airport, and Blake was watching Allie at the airport, and The Second and The Third were also at the airport along with and the two men from the Mexican cartel.

And they all wanted the same thing—possession of the vial.

CHAPTER 53

More Sober Than Drunk

The Mexican had been hiding in a hotel room with a pot of dirt that would not grow anything. It had been several days, and he needed a shave and a shower. Several trays of dirty dishes from room service and a few empty liquor bottles were piled up by the door. He had put a Do Not Disturb sign on the outside doorknob because he did not want maids coming into his room. He was not sober, but he was not drunk either. He was in a kind of liquor-infused mental limbo, waiting for something to grow.

The vial lay on the coffee table, and by now, it was nearly empty. At first, he had sparingly used six drops. Then another six drops. As he drank more liquor, he was less careful as he kept adding the serum from the vial into the pot of dirt thinking that was what was needed.

He had fallen into a combination of being asleep and passing out, and he suddenly woke up being more sober than drunk. His sober mind reminded him that he had been instructed to turn the vial over to his superiors, and when he looked at the vial, he found, to his horror, that it was almost empty. They would kill him. He knew they would not take kindly to his explanation that he was testing the serum for them to see how it worked. Even he did not believe that explanation!

He decided he would have to take a chance and make a run for it. That was better than waiting for them to find him and kill him. He tried to think clearly, but he found his brain only wanted more alcohol. He stood still in the middle of the room and closed his eyes so that he could think, and in true alcoholic fashion, he decided that another drink of alcohol would most certainly clear his mind and give him a solution to his problem. He opened his eyes and raised the bottle to his lips.

It was the last thing he would remember.

CHAPTER 54

A Population Explosion

Allie sat in the airport terminal and decided she was in a conundrum. She laughed out loud at the word. Conundrum. Blake had walked her to the section of the airport where the gate was for her departure to Kensington; however, he was not allowed to enter the waiting area, so they had said their goodbyes and exchanged phone numbers for future conversations.

Allie had tried to call The Third, but no one answered, so then she tried to call his friend, Lenny, but no one answered there either. So Allie made the decision to complete the rest of the trip to Kensington. She would meet Lenny and tell him what had happened, and then Lenny could pass that information on to The Third. Allie would then book a flight to Miami and consider this trip as a weird kind of vacation and holiday and adventure.

Life can be weird sometimes, she thought and decided this adventure would be one to pass on to her family. Normally, her life was very pragmatic in that she went to work each day, and then she went home where she followed her own little everyday habits with her cat, Oreo. Each week was almost the same as all the other weeks, and so this trip was a change from her regular daily habits. It had certainly been an adventure.

Then she thought of Blake, and that was a "plus" as she was certain they would keep in contact. It gave her a warm feeling that he would become a friend from this adventure. Allie thought Blake had left the terminal heading for his home in Seattle; however, she did not know he was still in the airport watching over her and hovering just out of her line of sight.

Blake knew Allie no longer had the vial because the Mexican had attacked her and made off with it, but Blake felt that she could still be in danger, and so he patiently watched over her and waited. He had purchased a ticket from Seattle to Kensington on a later flight than Allie. He knew she would be spending a few days there, and so he determined he would follow her until she safely returned to her home in Florida. He knew he was already caring far too much for her. While he worked for the United States government, he still had the freedom to move about the country at will when not on assignment. His goal was to negotiate and present a chance for the United States to take an active part in its distribution. While the vial was no longer physically present, Allie, and her safety, was now his top priority. She was his contact to the owner of the vial, so Blake stayed silent in the shadows.

It would seem as if the sleepy little town of Kensington situated just below the Arctic Circle was having a population explosion of sorts. It rarely had any visitors, and so anyone in the town who did not live there was immediately watched by all the townspeople. Allie and Blake and The Second and The Third and the two new Mexicans had all arrived within days of each other, and the gossip mills were running wild. And whether they knew it or not, the new arrivals all had the same interest—the vial and its contents. And the two Mexicans had an additional goal. Find the other Mexican who had apparently disappeared from the face of the earth.

Find him and you would find the vial of life. Lenny had no idea how much time had passed. He had given up his body to the couch, and it had rewarded him with a deep, satisfying sleep. It was the kind of sleep that a body craved when it needed to heal itself, and Lenny's body had received a blow to the head so severe that it almost bruised the brain, and that blow had resulted in his amnesia.

CHAPTER 55

Keep the Music Coming

Life and activities back at Whispering Palms had been so coordinated by Allie's excellent planning that Jim had no problem in allowing the different events planned to go forward. He had hired a "temp" who was a person who had stepped in and taken Allie's place in her absence. The temp was a very large, rather obese woman who seemed to immediately identify and blend in with the residents. She called bingo. She dealt blackjack. She set up tables and chairs for the activities. And she even tried to lead the exercise classes for the residents with the unspoken understanding that she could not bend and jump or even begin to lead them as Allie had done. She was inventive, however, and she found two residents who had addictively followed Allie's exercise classes and convinced them to lead the others while she kept the counts and the music coming. Still, Allie's absence was felt by everyone, and each hour that went by without a word from her gave everyone the chilling fear that something terrible must have happened to her.

Jim was at a loss as to how to proceed in the absence of an employee. He did not even inform his corporate office of his missing activities director, because he had expected her to appear with a completely plausible explanation. Between himself and the temp, they had not skipped a beat in presenting all the scheduled events, but Jim was very aware that this arrangement could not last. He had to admit he was at a complete loss as to how to proceed. And he was really beginning to feel a bone-chilling fear that something horrible must have happened to Allie. He literally felt sick when he had those thoughts. While murders and disappearances are in the news every day, we rarely give them a second thought because it was not happening in our world. It was not someone we knew. And yet, now there was an absence in their world of Whispering Palms. And it was someone they knew. It was their beloved Allie.

Still, Jim had faith in the person he knew as Allie. She would never just leave. And as far as he knew, she was not even involved in a relationship. But Jim had to admit to himself that an employer would only know that which an employee allowed them to know about their personal and private life. Her paycheck sat on her desk, unclaimed. He had picked it up, and it sat in his desk, waiting to be claimed by its owner. Jim had checked with her landlord and the church she attended and the cousin she had listed as a family contact, and no one knew why Allie had disappeared.

Jim had noticed that Mr. Freedman Carver III had not been attending any scheduled events, and when he checked further, it appeared that he was not even in the building. He had not been taking any meals, but neither had he informed the office that he would be absent for a time. The residents were expected to alert the office if they were to be away on vacation or family trips, but Mr. Carver had not done this. Jim had observed that the father and son occasionally would go out together, but it appeared to be just for a visit, taking a walk or sharing a meal. So it appeared that Mr. Carver and Allie were out of the facility at the same time, but Jim only noted this as a coincidence, and he gave it no further thought.

He heard himself sigh, and he realized that he was constantly stressing himself with the worry about a missing employee, and he was at a total loss as to how to proceed. He pressed his fingers against his temples as if to banish the headache that always presented itself when he thought of Allie and her sudden disappearance. *How can someone just up and disappear?* he thought, and yet he knew it happened every day. It was just that it had never happened to someone he knew. This time the sigh that escaped his throat sounded more like a sob, and he surprised himself, recognizing the feeling that he wanted to cry like a baby. He did not fight the feeling.

Jim sat and let the tears of fear and frustration fall before he composed himself and went back to his work.

CHAPTER 56

Do Not Disturb

The two hit men from Mexico had no trouble in finding one of the men who had been assigned to get the vial from Allie. Once in Seattle, they canvassed the main hotels, and having successfully bribed a few of the hotel front desk employees, they had the room numbers that had Do Not Disturb signs on them. It was an easy feat to wait until the wee hours of the morning to enter the rooms, and usually they just found couples who were having affairs outside of their marriages. They would then terrify the occupants and take their money and jewelry. They never harmed their victims who were so traumatized by the experience that they would disappear into the night, never reporting the incidents to the hotel.

They were down to only two more rooms on the main floor, and they approached the last of the two hotel suites with great caution. If the missing Mexican was in one of the rooms, he might have used his training to rig the door to set off a small explosive that would envelop the immediate area with a powder that was akin to pepper spray. This would give the occupant a few seconds to escape through a window or an adjacent suite.

They slid a collapsible camera mounted on a long, thin rod underneath the door, which showed them the stacks of dishes piled there, and the microphone on the camera did not detect any sound. This told them that there was probably only one occupant inside and not a couple. Next, they used the information they had obtained from bribing the front desk employees to determine that the suites on either side were occupied by couples and could not be used in an escape attempt. Finally, they used an electromagnetic device that was capable of silently releasing the electric key that locked the door. Placed against the lock, it would identify the numbers that held the lock in place, and a red light would show that the lock had been broken and that the door would easily open. The men were highly skilled in this type of entry. They positioned themselves in the hallway outside the door. Slowly and silently, they used the device to turn the doorknob, and the door soundlessly released itself from the lock. They waited. There was no motion from inside the room. Using a thin probe made of strong but soft rubber, they gently pushed against the door, and it gave way, opening to the hallway entrance inside the room. The intense blackness told them that the drapes were drawn, and the only light inside the room came from under the door of the bathroom. They could hear a hoarse repetitive sound recognizing it as heavy breathing coming from only one person. They were trained to move silently but quickly, and as one, they entered the suite, and both men stood still as they let their eyes adjust to the lack of light in the room. The bed was unmade with no one in it, and they could see the outline of a body that had been sitting in a lounge-type chair with an empty liquor bottle on its side on the floor. Rasping breaths emitted from the body, indicating the owner was well into an alcohol-induced sleep and would not be easily aroused by hearing a sound. The two men skirted the room noting a gun lying on a coffee table, and beside it lay the vial of life. They had found their associate, and he had the vial.

The most telling thing in the room was not the man nor the vial but the pot of dirt that sat defiant with no growth. One of the men silently moved to the door to close and lock it, leaving the Do Not Disturb sign on the doorknob. They did not want to be disturbed as they prepared to wait until they could rouse the room occupant from his drunken haze, and they would, not so gently, interrogate him to find out all he knew. Once that was accomplished, they would, again soundlessly, relieve him of his life breath. He'd be a shell of a body that could never again taste the joy of life. They took the vial and the information they had gained, and within a few hours, left the hotel with their new objective.

And her name was Allie.

CHAPTER 57

Get the Hell Out of Dodge

Allie, the Second and the Third, Blake, and soon the two Mexicans were all about to converge on Lenny's house, and no one knew the others were coming. From the beginning the vial of life had been the driving force, and while that remained true, some of the participants were now dealing with the added knowledge that their personal safety might be in jeopardy.

Allie was the total innocent in the equation, and The Second and The Third were one step away as these three were not armed with any weapons except their understanding that the vial presented a unique hope that it would one day bring hunger and famine to a worldwide standstill. The two Mexican cartel members were at the other end of the spectrum having already committed a murder in the search of the vial. Blake was armed, but he was plotting a different direction to the vial as his path was to convince Allie to turn over the vial to him so the United States would control its future.

And then there was Lenny who was now the focal point as all these people were approaching his home. If Lenny had not suffered a fall that caused him to have amnesia, he might have had the good sense to "get the hell out of Dodge," as the saying goes, but he was now mentally handicapped, and he could barely function. His home was, to him, his protection from the world until he could get his memory back, and so he hunkered down in his basement where, among his scientific paraphernalia, he was reading through his papers, searching for knowledge about himself.

At the Seattle airport, Allie waited to, once again, board an airplane on the last leg of her adventure. Her thoughts were on Blake as she was beginning to realize that she could be capable of having deeper feelings for him than just a friend. This last airplane ride to Kensington would be a lonely one without him across the aisle to talk to, and so she boarded the plane feeling alone and a little sad. She did not know that he was watching her from the terminal, wishing that he could somehow be on that same plane because he did not want her to be out of his sight.

The two Mexican cartel men had the money behind them to do whatever it took to get the vial from Allie, and they were also at the Seattle airport, but they were in the process of chartering a plane. Their interrogation of the drunken cartel agent had given them the information they needed to follow Allie, and they were on their way to Kensington.

The Second and The Third had already reached the Kensington airport and had managed to successfully rent a car. With their luggage stuffed into the back of a very small, very old sedan, The Second was trying to use their Google Map application on his phone to make their way to Lenny's home. The Second gave The Third his phone with the instructions to follow the map while he drove. Unfortunately, the only rental car available was a stick shift, and it had been at least thirty years or more since The Second had driven, let alone manipulate a gear shift and a clutch. He managed to coax the car into first gear and then second, but the jerky style of their forward motion resembled that of something from a comic movie.

Meanwhile, Lenny had adjusted to his memory lapse to the point where he understood his amnesia problem was a temporary thing. He knew that time would help the healing, but his pragmatic scientific training told him that he could help the process along by reading and studying things that pertained to his history. Stored in the basement were papers and filings of all his personal records, and so he fixed himself a sandwich with a large pitcher of milk and headed down the basement stairs. Kensington was such a small town, and as Lenny had no neighbors close to his house, he never locked his home.

This habit would almost prove to be his undoing.

CHAPTER 58

Changing Gears

The two Mexican cartel agents were trained to make decisions about their given instructions, and once that was done, to move quickly toward their assignment, and this occasion was no different. Their swiftness in charting a private plane allowed them to arrive in Kensington almost at the same time as The Second and The Third. They had wired ahead and, upon landing, had a rental car brought out to their plane. Their previous interrogation had given them Lenny's home address, and they wasted no time in pointing their car in that direction, and they easily passed the rental car of the father and the son.

Back at the Seattle airport, Blake had played a hunch and was able to speak to the airline employee handling the boarding of Allie's flight to Kensington. At first, the boarding agent had indicated that the flight was full; however, some smooth talking along with a considerable bribe netted Blake a seat at the back of the plane. He was the last one to board, and Allie, seated near the front of the plane, paid no attention to the late passenger. Blake always carried a few accessories and makeup, and he had given himself a scroungy-looking five o'clock shadow, and he wore a woolen cap pulled down over his head. He looked like a traveler who spent a lot of time in the woods, and he used his newspaper as another way to hide his identity. As the plane taxied out to the end of the runway, he settled down into his seat and did his best to blend into the interior of the plane looking like one of the many rugged passengers traveling to just below the Arctic Circle.

*****

The Second was sweating heavily as he fought the twisting and jerking movements of the rental car as he desperately tried to remember how to change gears without stripping the engine of its transmission. The Third was petrified that his father would somehow kill them both as they tried to drive to Lenny's house, and his assignment to help with the navigation was not helping their cause. A rental car raced past them, causing The Second to swear in frustration. Had he known that the car that passed them carried the two Mexican cartel agents, he would most certainly have used an entirely different set of swear words.

It was a short drive of fifteen minutes to Lenny's house, and the two Mexicans wisely circled the property, casing the area and finding the best place to park the car so it would not be seen from the house. They parked in the shadows to observe the home as they methodically changed their clothing so that everything they wore was black. They double-checked their firearms and made sure the knives they carried were within easy reach if needed. They had one last chore to do, and that was to contact their handlers to receive their instructions to advance and enter Lenny's house.

In the basement, Lenny had arranged an overhead lamp so that it gave him a singular light as he looked through his files. His usual custom was to have a radio tuned to an FM station that played his favorite records as the sound filled the silence of being alone in his house.

*****

As the plane slowly descended, Allie peered out of the window and was astonished to see that the city of Kensington was more like a very small village of Kensington. *Good heavens,* she thought. *And I had visions of a few days of sightseeing. It is so small it would only take…*

She paused to think, and she laughed out loud as she pictured herself walking from one end of the tiny town to the other in less than an hour.

Allie took out her compact mirror and touched up her hair and makeup, and she was glad that Lenny would be meeting her as she was looking forward to giving him greetings from his friend, The Third. She was wearing the red jacket that she had mentioned in the message she had sent him so he would recognize her. She sat back in the seat and buckled her seat belt as the flight attendant was advising everyone to do, and her overwhelming thought was that she was glad to see this northern trip was coming to an end so she could begin the trip back to her Miami home.

*****

Lenny was so engrossed in reading through his files, searching for clues to his identity, that he was oblivious to the sound of his front door opening and closing, and just like that, the two Mexicans were inside his home. They swiftly went through every room and realized that Lenny must be downstairs as they could hear the music drifting up the basement stairs. One man went down the basement steps while the other stayed upstairs, and both had their guns drawn. Lenny's peripheral vision warned him of motion beside him, and he looked up to find himself staring into a gun barrel. He was so surprised that he screamed, startling the Mexican who screamed back at him to put his hands up in the air. Lenny slowly raised his arms. The Mexican growled at him, "Where's the vial?"

Lenny replied, "Vial? What vial?"

The Mexican said, "You know what vial. The vial from your scientist friend."

Lenny said, "No, I don't know." Anxious to say something to please this man with a gun, Lenny pointed to the papers in his hand and said, "I forgot. But now I know. I am Lenny. My name is Lenny."

"Great," growled the Mexican. "And my name is Santa Claus. There is a girl coming to give you a vial." Lenny was looking at both men and their guns, and he shook his head and said, "I do not know about any vial. I had a headache, and I could not remember, but now I know that I am Lenny."

The Mexican who was upstairs could not hear the conversation, and he impatiently called down, "Come on. Bring that guy up here where we can both watch him." Lenny and the Mexican climbed the stairs with Lenny clutching his passport and his glass of water. Once upstairs, one of the men pushed him toward a kitchen stool and said, "Sit." Lenny obeyed and sat.

One of the men said, "We should tie him up." The other man sarcastically said, "Tie him up? I did not bring my rope. Do you have any rope?" The other man, missing the sarcasm, said, "Well, no. But we need to keep him here because the girl is supposed to bring him the vial."

The first man pointed his gun at Lenny and said, "When is the girl coming with the vial?"

Lenny said, "I told you. I do not know about any vial. I do not know about any girl. I cannot remember. And please do not point that gun at me. It makes me very nervous."

"Yeah, well, it makes me nervous too when you won't tell me about the girl and the vial," growled the Mexican.

There was an awkward silence. Lenny said, "Would you like something to drink? I have cold water." Lenny held up his glass.

Both men looked at him. One of the men said, "Yeah. I would like some."

The other man said, "Oh, for heaven's sake. This is not a tea party."

Just then the phone rang, and all three jumped in surprise. One man said, "He should answer it," pointing at Lenny. "Maybe it is the girl." The phone was an old-fashioned rotary phone, and he pushed it toward Lenny and said, "So answer it and don't say anything."

Lenny said, "How can I answer it if I don't speak?"

Getting increasingly aggravated, the man said, "Oh, for heaven's sake. I mean, do not say anything about us being here." The phone rang again. "Answer it! Wait. I want to put it on speakerphone," growled the man closest to him, and he pushed a button. Lenny slowly picked it up and said, "Hello. Lenny here." He grinned when he said his name and then repeated, "I am Lenny."

It was The Third on the phone, and he said, "Yes, Lenny. I certainly expected you to be there. My father and I have a rental car, and we are driving to your house. We should be there in about fifteen minutes."

The man closest to Lenny reached over and put his hand over the receiver and said, "Tell him you're not home."

"But I am at home. They know I am here."

"I mean, tell him you were just leaving and for them to come back another time."

Lenny shook his head and said, "Why would I tell him that?"

"Because," growled the man, "Because I'M TELLING YOU TO SAY THAT."

The other man said, "Wait up. The man on the phone just said, '*We're here.*' Maybe the girl is with him, and she has the vial."

"Ah, good thought," said the first man. "Okay. Tell them to come ahead, and you will leave the front door open, and they should just come in."

Lenny shook his head "no," and the man shoved the gun right up in front of Lenny's face and said, "Tell him!" Lenny removed his hand from the receiver and said, "I'll leave the front door open so you can come in."

"Perfect," said the voice on the speakerphone. "See you soon," and the click on the phone indicated he had hung up. Lenny put the receiver back in its cradle.

"So, who are those people?" growled one of the men closest to Lenny.

Lenny shook his head and said, "I honestly do not know. I told you I cannot remember." The phone rang again, and one man said, "Good lord, this is a busy place." Lenny answered the phone

"Hello."

"Hi, Lenny. This is Allie. My plane just landed, and I am going to pick up my luggage, and I'll meet you by the main entrance in the terminal. Oh, and I am wearing a red jacket."

Lenny did not say anything. After a slight pause, they heard her say, "Hello. Lenny? Are you still there?" The man closest to Lenny waved his gun at him and whispered in his ear, "Tell her to take a taxi here."

"Yes. I am here, Allie. Listen, can you take a taxi here? I am kind of tied up at the moment." Lenny kind of chuckled at his own joke.

"Oh, sure thing. I can do that. I will get a taxi, and I will see you soon." Allie hung up the phone. The man took the phone out of Lenny's hand and put it back on the cradle. "So, are you expecting any more phone calls?"

"No," said Lenny. "I really do not know. I cannot remember anything, and I have a headache."

"Yeah, well, I have a headache too, and now, it's because of you! And all your visitors. So, in fifteen minutes we are expecting a man to drive up here. And then we are also expecting a taxi from the airport to drive up here with a girl."

Lenny said, "Apparently so. I really cannot remember."

The man said, "Well, remember this," and he waved the gun in Lenny's face. "This has a way of making people remember."

CHAPTER 59

A Celebration of Sorts

The Second was getting a little better at changing gears as they slowly but surely drove toward Lenny's house. Both men were tired, and the thought of getting something to eat and a soft bed was the driving singular force that kept them going.

When they were crunched inside the small airplane, The Third had taken advantage of that time to think, and he was sure that sending the vial to Lenny had been the best thing to do at the time. However, he was beginning to realize that time was not their best friend. He sensed that they were not the only people chasing after the vial, and his memories of shadowy men hovering around his residence back at Whispering Palms were beginning to haunt him. He also realized that Allie was out there, somewhere in the vast world, and he was the one responsible for sending her all the way to Lenny's house. And so, he quietly sat in the very old, very small sedan that his father was attempting to drive and did his best to maintain his composure as he willed them all to safely arrive at Lenny's and be that much closer to having this trip over.

*****

Allie looked around the reasonably small terminal at Kensington, and seeing the area where the taxis parked, she picked up her luggage and walked in that direction. She realized that she was experiencing a new chapter in her adult life, that of being alone in an entirely new and different situation and making mature decisions. While it was mentally exhilarating, she also wanted it to be over so that she could return to her job at Whispering Palms and especially to her cat, Oreo.

It was something of a dichotomy because the entire experience seemed to have taken a long time; however, it also felt as if it had not been a long period of time in her life. Allie entertained both thoughts as she prepared to make the final leg of the trip to meet the scientist friend, Lenny, and give him the vial that was now nestled inside her makeup kit. She had decided it was probably best to carry it in her purse rather than wear it. She wondered how The Third was doing back at Whispering Palms, and she made a promise to herself to call him as soon as she met Lenny and made the delivery.

Back at Lenny's, the two Mexicans were arguing between each other as to how to proceed. They had their guns on Lenny; however, the two phone calls that had happened while they were there informed them that soon there would be more people in Lenny's house, and then they would be outnumbered. They agreed to split up with one man hiding in the basement while the other man would patrol the main floor of the house. One Mexican was suggesting that they should immediately tie Lenny up and leave him in the basement, and that way they would have control of the house when the others arrived. The other Mexican argued that they should use Lenny to lure the people arriving into the house, and then, once they were inside, they could use surprise and brute force to overwhelm everyone.

Listening to their discussion, Lenny decided he did not want to allow them to take control of him and his house. While he still had the memory loss, he was getting what he determined were flashbacks that were allowing him to remember who he was. He had noticed that when he acted as if he did not comprehend what was going on, the two men tended to ignore him as they talked among each other. They put Lenny in the kitchen because it was a small room and had only one entrance door from the inside of the house. What it also had was utensils and a drawer that held small, sharp kitchen knives that Lenny used for pealing vegetables. He leaned against the drawer and was able to pull it out far enough out so that he could lift several of the paring knives out of the drawer. He was able to slip one inside each shoe and drop one into every pocket in his jeans. Lenny was not an athlete, and indeed, he could be described as short and dumpy in stature; however, he was very smart. He knew that his best chance of overpowering them was diversion and to make them think he was basically useless and not a threat to them, and so he set out to appear that way.

*****

The Second finally had gained a certain amount of control over the stick shift in the car, and he relaxed a little as his driving improved, and he maneuvered the rental car down the road. The Third began to relax more too with the smoother ride produced by his father, and so he began going over what he should do once they got to Lenny's house. He certainly had not expected that he would have been the one to make the trip to Lenny's, but here he was. He wondered where Allie was on her journey to Lenny's house. He smiled when he envisioned how surprised she would be to see him there too. It would be like a mini family reunion, and he decided that one thing he would do would be to take everyone out to a restaurant for dinner. It would be a celebration of sorts that they and the vial were all safely at Lenny's house.

*****

Lenny waited. The Mexicans waited. Lenny was in the small kitchen area. The Mexicans were in the main living room that had a window that looked out over the road that led into Lenny's property. No one wanted to be the first one to move, and so they all remained as if they were cemented into place. It was as if the actual air inside the house was so still that, to the three men, it felt as if you could reach out and touch it.

And so, they all waited.

CHAPTER 60

Street Smarts

At first, it was not even noticeable. One seeing it would think it was possibly air that hovered over the earth that had become so hot that, after a rise in temperature, you could see waves of air shimmering in place. Then, ever so slightly, a small brownish cloud appeared. The cloud grew bigger and moved a little faster, and suddenly, the cloud became a small dark-colored car that was driven by The Second. The car was traveling on a tinder-dry dirt road, which, to first appearance, seemed to be a ribbon that turned into a swirling stretch of dust that encompassed everything.

There was no way The Second and The Third could have announced their arrival any better if they tried. To the Mexicans watching the cloud car get closer and closer, they experienced a mixture of great anticipation and paralyzing fear. It was the latter that was their greatest enemy because it is fear that makes most men begin to doubt and question themselves in a time of overpowering stress.

Lenny could not have spoken and explained his emotional status, but he knew he was regaining his mental faculties. With his lifelong scientific training, he went inside his mind to focus his thoughts, and it was as if he had shone a flashlight inside his skull, and he was watching a movie.

While the Mexicans could not be classified as having a great deal of intelligence, that did not mean that they were not smart. They both had what is referred to as street smarts, meaning they could be ruthless when they found themselves in situations where they felt that they were backed into a corner and had to come out fighting to survive. The Mexicans had reached that place. People were approaching Lenny's house who might have the capability to get to the vial before they could. Lenny, operating on his gut-level instinct, immediately read their change of attitude and became their perfect hostage.

"Oh damn," he whined, "damn, damn, damn! With more people here, we will not be able to use the storm shelter hiding place. No, no, no. We cannot use it. Too many people. Too many. Too many!" He paced around in a little circle, adding to his look of being someone who was losing it, and he kept mumbling to himself. One of the Mexicans walked over to him and slammed him across his forehead with his gun, causing Lenny to drop to his knees. Lenny literally saw stars, but he had enough presence of mind to continue his mumbling. Lenny considered rolling on the floor toward them, hopefully causing them both to fall, but each man still had their gun, and Lenny decided he could not risk it, so he continued whispering his mumbling to appear as if he was still out of it.

The Mexican who had hit him continued to escalate his panic mode while the other man took him by the shoulders and shook him violently. On the floor, Lenny was trying, in vain, to move away from them. Suddenly, they heard a car horn honking, and both Mexican men moved to the dining room windows. The Second had succeeded in parking the car in the driveway and had decided to honk his horn to alert Lenny that they had arrived. While one Mexican continued to panic, the other went into action. He opened a small door within the kitchen that led to an enclosed pantry, and he dragged and shoved Lenny inside and slammed the door and turned the doorknob to lock it. He moved to the kitchen sink, and filling a glass with water, he threw it into the face of the other Mexican and while the man was temporarily stunned, he slapped his face twice and yelled at him to snap out of it. Apparently, it worked as the Mexican immediately regained his composure and said, "Basement." Both men bolted and dove for the basement stairs, falling over each other to get to the bottom. And then there was silence in the kitchen.

The Second and The Third had parked the car, and each was struggling with their suitcase as they prepared to go to the front door of Lenny's house. The Second dropped his suitcase and strong-armed his son, causing him to stumble and lose his grip on his luggage. The Third was tired and frustrated, and this action by his father caused him to lose his patience and yell at The Second.

"What in God's name are you doing?" The Third yelled. "We need to get into the house and you're not helping."

The Second adopted the soothing tone that he used with his son when he felt he was the adult in the room and was making decisions for both. "I know. I know, but we are not certain we are going to stay with Lenny. We might have to go to a hotel, so let us leave our suitcases in the car."

The Third wanted to talk back to his father and tell him that Lenny would most certainly have them stay with him, but he was too tired to resist, so he just said, "Fine. Fine. Let us just get inside and decide then."

The Third shook his head from side to side as if he was the "adult in charge," and The Second nodded his head up and down as if he was the adult in charge, and both men momentarily looked like a version of the little Weeble-Wobble statues you can put on your car dashboard and watch their heads move. The Third broke their nodding competition and said "Let us get inside. I know Lenny will be really glad to see us."

If anyone had the ability to watch over the events happening at Lenny's house, they would have noted that everyone involved with something to do with the vial was arriving at the same place. They were the two Mexican men, Lenny; The Second, The Third, Allie, and Blake who was watching out for Allie at a distance.

It would be crowded.

CHAPTER 61

Cancellation Instructions

It was very quiet in the kitchen pantry, which was a good thing because Lenny had a horrendous headache; however, he needed the quiet time to try to think. He was experiencing memory flashbacks, which did not come with those written subtitles you get with foreign films, so it was like watching a movie with the sound turned down. He had figured that this was his home, and the two men were apparently thugs of some kind and wanted something from him. He knew they were dangerous. He did not know who the elderly man was who continued to appear in his memory, but he sensed he was a friend. He decided that remaining quiet was the best thing he could do, and so Lenny sat on the floor of the kitchen pantry. He closed his eyes not to sleep but to give what was left of his memory the energy and space to work. And so, Lenny waited.

The Second and The Third were at Lenny's front door and had pushed the doorbell several times, but no one came to let them in. The Second was tired from driving the rental car, and he needed desperately to get to a bedroom with a bed so he could rest. The Third was tired as well, but he had developed the serum in the vial, and he had given it to Allie to deliver to Lenny, and he felt that responsibility was heavy on his mind. He used both hands to bang loudly on Lenny's front door, and his level of frustration was turning to fear that something terrible had happened to his friend, Lenny.

*****

Allie slowly wandered over to the section of the airport that advertised taxi service when she suddenly realized it would be a good thing to visit yet again another ladies' room and freshen up. *Good time to add one more airport ladies' room to my list*, she thought with a smile.

Blake found himself again following Allie to a restroom, and he was beginning to wonder if this assignment had reached its apex and if he should contact his American handlers to see if they wanted him to abandon and pull back from his observation of Allie. It was a choice he hoped would not be given, but there was always a point in surveillance when continuation needed to be questioned and revalued. He hoped he would not receive cancellation instructions, and so he patiently waited and watched.

*****

Finally, The Third came to the end of his patience, and he reached out and turned the handle of the front door only to find that it easily gave way, and the door swung open. Both men were frozen in place, and neither moved. Finally, The Second regained his composure and said, 'Let's find your friend Lenny," and he stepped inside the house.

Down in the basement, the two Mexicans realized that they were out of sight of the people approaching the house, but it also meant they could not see or hear anything that was happening upstairs. And they did not know how long the man they had locked in the pantry would stay quiet. They had the advantage of being aware, but also the disadvantage of being out of the range of vision. Lenny's house became the focal point of all the people who wanted the vial to be safely in their hands.

All of it being equal, it was a toss-up as to who would be successful.

CHAPTER 62

Door Number Two

Once inside yet another airport restroom, Allie went through her usual habits and found herself once again looking at herself in the mirror. Suddenly, she felt a series of cold shivers overtake her body, and she froze in place with the gut-level feeling that something was wrong. Up to this point, the experience had been one of a lark. A kind of adolescent adventure that she had taken and not given it much thought. Her mind again went to Blake, and she found she missed him terribly as he had allowed her to enjoy the traveling. But now, she was experiencing a kind of fear that caused her to feel hot and cold at the same time. She opened her purse to take out her makeup kit, and she glimpsed what appeared to be a soft light. A kind of shimmer. It was then that her memory kicked in, and she remembered. At the last minute when she had put The Third into a taxi to take him back to Whispering Palms, he had reached out, and taking her hand in his, he had slipped a small envelope into her palm. His eyes bored into hers, and he said "Allie, this is for you to use if you ever feel alone." Allie had taken it, and it fell into her purse as she had assured him that she would be just fine and that she was not afraid to fly alone. Now, with the hot and cold chills running up and down her spine, she reached into her purse and opened the envelope because she was terribly aware that she did indeed feel alone.

*****

Down in the basement, the Mexicans heard the front door open, and then the sound of footsteps echoed across the ceiling of their basement room. In the kitchen pantry, Lenny's eyes opened wide as he heard the front door open and the muffled sound of footsteps as someone entered the house. The three people inside the house also knew that they had visitors. The two visitors to the house were looking to find The Third's friend Lenny. For all five people, it became a moment they would all look back on as the beginning of the time they would all make decisions they wished they could have changed.

Allie had opened the envelope and found a smaller version of the vial that The Third had placed around her neck back at Whispering Palms. This smaller vial was also on a delicate chain making it appear as if it was jewelry. Allie did not hesitate but lifted it to her chest and closed the clasp. Strangely, she immediately felt less alone. She looked inside the envelope hoping to find a note of instructions, but the envelope was empty.

It was as if the vial itself, which felt cool against her skin, held all the power that she needed to complete her journey, so Allie splashed some water on her face, combed her hair, put on some lipstick, and looking at herself in the mirror, decided to enjoy the last leg of this adventure. She looked forward to meeting Lenny, and it would only happen if she took a taxi and made the trek to his house. Suddenly, it felt as if she needed to hurry to complete this adventure, and so she closed her purse, took one last look at herself in the mirror, and went out into the terminal to find an available taxi to take her to Lenny's house.

Blake was almost nodding off when his vision alerted him to the picture of Allie walking briskly out of the ladies' room. Blake could hardly believe his eyes as he saw that Allie once more wore a vial on a chain around her neck. It was smaller than the vial that had been stolen from her, but it was the same vial of life. Allie was moving so quickly that she was already out of his sight as she disappeared into the busy life of the airport terminal. Blake silently cursed himself for his actions in losing sight of her, and he strode out into the sea of tourists and headed in the direction he had seen her walk. He could not afford to lose her now, and he felt an unaccustomed knot in his stomach of fear as he realized he might lose her and his chance to get the vial itself.

As the taxi smoothly pulled away from the airport terminal, Allie was delighted to have had the good fortune to come across a taxi parked at the curb. It was obvious that it was the last available airport taxi, and the driver nearly fell over himself as he seated his new fare inside the back seat. With an obvious practiced move, he fell into the driver's seat and, throwing the car into gear, pulled away before Allie could give him directions. She was on her way to Lenny's house, and she had her hand on the minivial as she felt an excited turn of her thoughts as she was so close to completing her trip. Her smile seemed to light the back seat of the taxi as she gave the driver Lenny's address. She was almost there.

*****

The Second and The Third stood in the entrance hallway of Lenny's house, uncertain as to what to do next. The Third called out. "Lenny, we are here. It is my father and I. Sorry we barged in. We tried to call to let you know we were coming and…" His voice trailed off as he realized he seemed to be talking to an empty house.

The Second said, "Do you think he is out shopping? Or maybe even gone away for a few days?"

The Third said, "From what I know of Lenny's shopping habits, he likes to call from home and have things delivered. And I have never known him to go away. Not even for a few days." The Third tried once again, and he called out, "Lenny. It is Freedman. I am here with my father, and we have just come from the airport." He paused. Silence. "Lenny?"

The Second said, "Well, it seems he is not here, and we are, so what shall we do?"

The Third said, "Let us look around. I am sure he has a spare room, and we can bring our luggage in and wait until he gets home."

The Third said, "Well, first things first, and I have need of a restroom." The two men tentatively moved down the hallway and into the house.

Lenny could certainly hear them as could the Mexicans lurking in the basement, and neither were sure that they should speak out loud, so everyone kept silent. Lenny had another flashback, and his returning memory told him that this Freedman was his good friend.

The Second found a bathroom off the hallway, and The Third wandered into a room that was obviously a bedroom not used by anyone. The bed suddenly looked so inviting and he threw himself across the length of it and let out a huge sigh as lying prone relieved his back of its job of holding him upright. He realized he was one deep breath away from going to sleep, and he took a deep breath, allowing his core to relax and unwind. He did not want to move. He was on the very edge of falling asleep when his father barged into the room, and with a demanding voice said, "So, son, what shall we do now?"

The Third wanted to tell his father to just lie down and be quiet and go to sleep, but he said, "Let's just wait for an hour and see if Lenny did go out and comes home. After that hour, I have no idea. Yes, I do. Going to sleep would be a good idea."

His father said, "Yes, sleeping sounds like a fine idea, but first, I want to take stock of your friend Lenny's home so we know a little bit of the landscape," and so he turned and marched out to inspect the house.

The Third propped himself up on one elbow and watched his father march off, and he had two choices. Door number one, lie back down on the bed and go to sleep, or door number two, get up and follow his father. While The Third longed to stay on the bed, he could not have his father moving around Lenny's house snooping, so he chose door number two and reluctantly left the welcoming softness of the bed.

Down in the basement, the two Mexican hit men looked at each other to determine their next move. They were well versed in the art of silent communication, and they immediately agreed to let the man upstairs wander around. After all, he was one person, and they were two, and he did not know they were there. The odds were obviously on their side. And so, they silently waited.

In the kitchen pantry, Lenny also waited. He was not sure what he was waiting for. His head hurt terribly. He decided he was not good at waiting, and every fiber of his being called out for him to get up and move around. Doing that, getting up and moving around, involved planning. And his head hurt so much that even the slightest movement sends shards of pain streaking across the inside of his head. Even thinking hurt. He swore he could see lightning inside his head. When he was still…so still that one might think he was dead… when he was still, he could override the pain, and that seemed to be the most intelligent thing to do. And so, he closed his eyes and curled into a fetal position and lay very still. He was the master of what little pain there was, and so he concentrated on not moving and not thinking and just kind of existing in a little puddle on the floor.

Lenny lay very still. For the moment, he was in charge.

CHAPTER 63

Follow the Yellow Brick Road

The taxi was old, and it creaked as it bumped along the not very well-paved road. Allie could almost taste the feeling of coming to the end of a journey, and she listened to the creaking of the old car. Somehow she felt that it was apropos that she should find herself in an old car as she covered the last leg of this adventure. She could sense that she was getting a second wind for which she was grateful, and so, in true Allie fashion, she sat up a little straighter, smoothed out her clothing, and let her thoughts take her to thinking about her darling feline roommate, Oreo. She knew he would not go hungry or be without attention as Ms. Wilheim would make sure he was cared for. But Allie knew that Oreo would want to be with her. Beside her. Curled up in the fashion that cats do, accepting all the cooing words Allie would send in his direction as she gently and expertly rubbed his forehead and his ears and his neck and ran her fingers down his back. Cats "allow" us to massage them, and in return, they purr and stretch out and roll over and pull back into a fetal position all the while getting the very best in massaging while giving us the impression it was hard work for them to do that. And as humans, we delight in doing all that work to give a cat pleasure.

Back at Lenny's house, The Second was basically snooping. It was obvious that no one was home, but he was doing what humans often succumb to, which is snooping in a place that is not his. The Third was not at all interested in seeing Lenny's house as he wanted to find out where Lenny was and why he was not at home. The Second had come to the top of the basement stairs and had switched on the one light bulb that hung from the ceiling. There was absolutely no reason for him to go down the stairs, but he was snooping. The two Mexicans were huddled behind the chesterfield, and they could peer around it watching him come down the stairs. One man was content to have him slowly come down to stand on the basement floor. The other man wanted to immediately step out and attack him. With a hand on his partner's arm, he succeeded in holding him back, and when The Second turned his back on them to look at a far side of the basement, he stealthily stood, and raising his arm well above his head, he brought the barrel of the gun down firmly on the small bald spot on The Second's head with as much force as he could muster.

The Second literally saw stars as his brain reacted to the assault. His eyes rolled back into his head, and his knees collapsed first, giving way to his legs, and then the rest of him just folded up upon itself as he hit the floor unconscious. The more aggressive Mexican raised his gun as if to shoot him while the other pushed his arm away, shaking his head no. "He may know something," he whispered. "He came here after the vial. We need to have him alive." The other nodded his understanding and strode over to some window drapes and pulled off the rope holding it back, and pulling the arms of the man behind his back, he deftly tied several knots. Even though the man was out cold, the Mexican needed to satisfy his explosive nature, and he kicked him several times in the rib area and only stopped when the other Mexican pulled him back and said, "Another time, my friend. Another time. We need to get back upstairs so we can watch the front door."

Upstairs, The Third was oblivious to his father's absence as he was going through papers on Lenny's desk to see if he could find any information on where Lenny might be. He kept shaking his head and mumbling, "But he never goes out. Where can he be? I do not understand. Where can he be?"

Meanwhile, Allie's taxi was just pulling up at Lenny's house, and the driver parked beside the rental car. "Hmm," the driver said out loud to no one. "That there is a rental car, so it looks as if your friend has out-of-town visitors. Anyone you might know, missy?"

Allie hated that he called her missy as if he knew her, and she was not pleased that he was apparently trying to get personal information from her. The thought flew through her mind that his nosiness had just cost him a couple of dollars of his tip.

"I wouldn't know," Allie said with an icy tone to her words as she handed him the fare reaching over the front seat and immediately letting herself out of the back seat of the cab. She was beginning to realize that she had almost completed her journey, and she did not feel like making small talk with a nosy cab driver. She stood and looked at Lenny's house and thought, *Okay, Lenny. You are about to be the recipient of the vial of life entrusted to you by Freedman Carver the Third. I hope you are up to the responsibility*, and Allie walked the last few yards toward Lenny's front door, having no knowledge that she was walking into a danger zone.

*****

Blake was swearing to himself, which was something he rarely did, but he felt his frustration and anger with the situation rise as he had to stand and watch Allie's taxi drive away from the airport terminal. It was obvious to him that she had taken the last available taxi, and Blake would have to wait for another taxi to return looking for a new fare. It was moments like this that caused him to silently curse his job. Not everything was easy or fell into place, and it was the unknown happenings, like not having a taxi available, that could make or break an agent's assignment. All he could do was stand in the deserted taxi area and watch the taxi carrying Allie grow smaller and smaller as it disappeared down the road.

*****

Lenny's head was hurting less; however, he knew, by instinct, that the safest thing for him would be to stay huddled in the pantry. However, these men had come into his home with the obvious intent to do harm, and Lenny felt he could use his superior intelligence to find a way out of this situation. He closed his eyes and welcomed the darkness that appeared, and then he willed his mind to rise to the occasion with a solution. And so, Lenny lay quiet waiting for an answer.

Allie stood at the door, and taking a deep breath, she pushed the doorbell, immediately recognizing the chimes that pealed out "Follow the Yellow Brick Road" from the movie, *The Wizard of Oz*. She laughed out loud and thought, *Indeed*. She imagined she had been following a yellow brick road of her own, and she immediately felt a kinship with the house.

In the kitchen, Lenny heard his beloved "Wizard of Oz" doorbell chime out, and his mind suddenly lit up when he realized that the young lady that The Third had said would be arriving was most likely at his front door. Lenny knew that the Mexicans were probably not about to go to the door, so he slowly stood and headed in the direction of his front door.

Allie waited and listened, but all she heard was a huge silence as if the house was taking its time to answer. She pushed the doorbell again and was greeted with the chiming chords. Allie placed her hand on the doorknob, and though she expected it to be locked, she gently turned it to the right and was surprised when she felt a gentle click as the doorknob disengaged and the door silently swung open, and she was staring into the eyes of someone she knew.

In the basement, it had taken both Mexicans to drag Freedman Carver II across the floor. Dead weight is dead weight, and an ordinary human is extremely heavy when they are unconscious. They were both breathing heavily as they positioned him behind the chesterfield when the doorbell chimes rang out. Both men grabbed their guns and literally fell and tripped over The Second as they dove behind the couch. Had anyone been watching, it would have seemed to be a move taken from *The Three Stooges* movie. They heard the footsteps of The Third as he moved to go to the front door. It seemed that the traffic at Lenny's house was almost like Grand Central Station.

The Third had not noticed the disappearance of his father as he was searching through Lenny's paperwork, and suddenly, the silence of the house was filled with the musical notes of "Follow the Yellow Brick Road." He hesitated and then made an immediate decision to go and open the door, thinking it might be a food delivery that Lenny had ordered. He shuffled down the hallway to the front door when suddenly, silently the door swung open and he was looking into the eyes of someone he knew.

Both were stunned to see their friend in the doorway, and Allie broke the silence first as she laughed and laughed as she stepped forward to hug The Third who was not one to know much about hugs, and he stood stiff and silent with his mouth open. Allie continued to laugh only because the sudden scare had taken away her ability to talk, and so she gave in to the reaction of laughter.

Almost immediately, the two Mexicans appeared in the doorway, and Allie's laughter turned to screams as she watched as two men fall on top of The Third. Both Mexicans had pushed The Third to the floor in the hallway. Immediately, one of the men jumped up and dove at Allie, pushing her body up against the wall. This action caused Allie to freeze in place, and she could not move, but her ability to scream remained intact so she screamed with all her strength. The Mexican was growling at her to stop screaming or he would shoot her. Allie heard his warning and went silent, but she was young and agile, and the Mexican was older and out of shape. The Mexican tried to pull Allie inside the doorway, but in doing so, he stepped backward and fell over The Third who was being held down by the other Mexican.

Suddenly, Allie felt herself being pulled toward the inside of the house, and she started to fight back until she found herself looking into the eyes of Lenny. She had never met him, but her gut-level instinct told her he was a friend and not a foe, and so she pulled away from the pile of three men writhing on the floor and ran. They both ran. They ran through the house and down the basement stairs, and Lenny led them to a small doorway, and opening it, he pushed Allie inside and closed it behind them. It was pitch dark until Lenny reached up and pulled on a cord that led to a single light bulb hanging from the ceiling. The light barely illuminated the space, and he motioned for her to be quiet as he reached up to the door they had tumbled through and twisted the handle to lock it. They were both winded, and for a minute, all they could do was gasp for air.

Allie recovered first and, as she knew it was Lenny's house she had come to, she mouthed "Lenny?" And he shook his head to answer yes. Allie and Lenny were in a storm shelter that Lenny had built years ago, and behind them, they had left The Second, The Third, and two mad Mexicans.

For the moment, they were safe.

The long, dark sedan with tinted windows drove silently down the street, looking for all the world like something out of a horror movie. The driver expertly parked beside a rental car that was parked in the driveway. The car lights went dark, and then it just sat there. Inside, the lone occupant was speaking into a phone as he was pulling on a dark parka with a hood to cover his face and head. His assignment had been given to him through an office that handled only the most confidential matters. He understood that once he accepted the job, he would literally be on his own. He could not expect to receive any backup help if he ran into trouble, and sitting in the car outside of Lenny's house, he knew he had moved into that never-never zone.

CHAPTER 64

The Never-Never Zone

Inside Lenny's house, there were now two worlds. One was inhabited by the Mexican cartel members who had taken The Second and The Third as hostages, and the other world held Lenny and Allie who, for the moment, were huddled in a storm shelter deep inside the basement. Neither world was prepared to overtake the other, and so they sat and they waited. And they waited. Soon someone would have to move.

Lenny knew he had to tell Allie what had happened to him. He had an old tablet and pencil that he had kept in the storm shelter to keep track of the supplies he had stored there. He found that he could print. Cursive looked like a jumble of strange circles, but surprisingly, he could print quite well. And so, he started. Whispering and writing, he slowly told her of his friendship over the years with The Third. He managed to describe how he had fallen and totally lost his memory and how it was slowly returning. He ended with his description of the two men who had managed to come into his home. He did not know who they were, but he suspected they were following his friend The Third and his father, The Second, and finally, he said the contents of the vial must be the reason they were in his home.

Allie sat and listened and watched as Lenny struggled to print out why they were hiding in his basement. As the story unfolded, she became more and more overwhelmed as the enormity of his story presented itself. She was realizing that they were in grave danger, and her lark of an adventure was turning into a literal do-or-die situation. She was totally unprepared for it all, and she could only sit and look at Lenny and shake her head in wonderment. Lenny understood as he also had to adapt to the seriousness of their plight. And he had to deal with the terribly restrictive position of having amnesia that continued to send him flashbacks, some of which only added increased confusion. It was truly a case of the blind leading the blind.

*****

The Third had gone to answer the doorbell at Lenny's house, and he found himself looking into the eyes of the woman he had entrusted with the secret of the vial. That was the last thing he remembered. And the last thing The Second remembered was going down the basement stairs and looking around. Then everything went black.

So now the son, The Third, found himself lying on the basement floor with his hands bound behind his back beside his father who had obviously been knocked unconscious. *What on earth happened?* The Third thought. He assumed that they would have been safe inside Lenny's house, but it seemed they must have been followed by the same men who had searched his apartment at Whispering Palms. Then he thought about Allie and the fact that he was responsible for asking her for help. And where was Lenny? The Third could see that his father had obviously been hit on the head; however, his breathing was stable, so hopefully he would regain consciousness soon. Then a wave of guilt washed over him knowing that his father had been a victim of this horrible course of events.

The Third closed his eyes, and while men of his age and generation do not cry, he could not stem the flow of tears that surfaced and cascaded down his cheeks. He was not an evil man. He was just a simple man who loved science and who, after years and years of failures, had succeeded. He put together atoms and molecules that produced a serum that made things grow. Really grow! He did not care for money, but he did care that others wanted to take the serum for the money it would bring on the world market. And it was that single thought that coursed through his mind, giving him the strength to do whatever it would take to stop them. Mind you, at that moment, he was at a disadvantage being tied up and lying beside his father in Lenny's basement. But he would wait, and he would find an answer. Whatever these men decided to do with him, he would find the right moment to act. With this thought in mind, he knew he would need all his strength, both mentally and physically, and so he did the only thing he could. He pragmatically closed his eyes and willed himself to sleep so he would have the strength to be ready when it was needed.

Lenny had an analytical mind, even though it was presently steeped in confusion and various shades of amnesia. He found he could clearly think and analyze the moments of the present, and he knew that staying in the confines of his storm shelter may give them an immediate respite, but they could not stay there. Inside the storm shelter, he had no way of knowing what the men in his house were doing. While he had not the faintest idea how to fight against them, he also knew that he and Allie had to outwit them somehow. And to do that, they had to get back upstairs.

His fingers shook as he printed the words out so that Allie would understand. WE HAVE TO MOVE NOW. Allie read the message and shook her head in agreement. Lenny reached up and pulled the string to turn off the single bulb, and he hesitated long enough for his eyes to adjust to the sudden darkness. Slowly he twisted the lock and lifted the door so they could climb out of the shelter, and moving as one, they reached the stairs.

Together they mounted the stairs going up into the house.

CHAPTER 65

The Blind Leading the Blind

What the Mexicans lacked in intelligence they excelled in street smarts, and each man instinctively moved into a mindset necessary to preserve their immediate situation. They had subdued the two men, and their next trophies would be the other man and the young woman who had disappeared and were hiding somewhere in the basement. They split up and moved silently toward the stairs leading to the basement. Each man took a side of the door. One man put up his hand to listen, and they heard the creaking of the stairs as Lenny and Allie made their way up toward the main floor. With the advantage of surprise, they waited until Lenny and Allie moved into the room, and moving as one, they easily overpowered the two unsuspecting people. Brandishing their guns, they forced Lenny and Allie back down the basement steps. Since they had discovered the drapes with all the tieback sashes, they had all the rope that they might need, and they worked quickly to tie up Lenny and Allie using their handkerchiefs to prevent them from being able to speak. So now the score was Mexicans, four. Everyone else, zero.

At this point, if anyone would have been keeping score, it may appear that the Mexicans were winning as they now had four people tied up. And one of those four people had a small vial hanging around her neck containing the vial sample. In their combined haste, they did not take time to examine Allie, and so they accomplished two things at once. They won, and they lost. They had the one thing they were seeking, the vial, but they did not know of its presence, and so they had won, but they also lost because of their ignorance.

In the basement, not only had The Third been power-sleeping while he lay tied up on the basement floor; when awake, he used his fingers to claw at the rope around his wrists. The Law of Average tells us that repetition is rewarded, and so it was that The Third was able to find and irritate the part of the rope holding the knot in place, and it fell away, freeing him to move. At first, he could not move as his muscles and tendons ignored him. They were handicapped from lack of use, and so it took the use of mental stimulation as The Third doggedly commanded his mind to zero in on individual muscles. It almost overwhelmed his ability to move his arms and legs, but "mind over matter" is a truism that cannot be ignored. And so, The Third used the railing to steady himself as he very slowly lifted his core to a sitting position. Then he leaned against the wall. Giving himself time to renew his energy level, he rested and waited. He gathered his legs underneath him, and using the railing for added leverage, he stood up. If anyone is counting, the count is now Mexicans, three. Everyone else, one.

The Third knew he had to leave immediately and could not stay beside his father, and so he reached down and brushed the hair away from his forehead and released the chord tying his hands behind his back. The Second stirred and opened his eyes. Just as he did that, he heard the Mexicans' footsteps overhead as they walked toward the basement stairs. There was no place to hide and no time as Lenny's basement door creaked to let them know it would soon open, and so The Third gave himself permission to, once again, lay on the basement floor, holding his hands behind his back. The Mexicans turned on the single light bulb and began their descent down the basement stairs. Allie and Lenny could only lie still and watch The Third as he joined them in the guise of being tied up. The count went back to Mexicans, four; everyone else, zero. At least for the moment.

CHAPTER 66

Fight or Flight

It was true the Mexicans did not have a plan, but they did have four people tied up in the basement, and to the two Mexicans, that was the equivalent of having money in the bank. And it seemed to them to be the time to make a withdrawal from their account of four. The overhead bulb was capable of only giving out enough light to create shadows, and so that fact helped to slow them down as they took each stair slowly and carefully. Neither man knew what they would do when they reached the basement floor, but each realized they must unanimously agree, and so they were solemn and silent until they stood on the basement floor.

Allie and Lenny were by the chesterfield by the far wall, and the father and son were lying almost on top of each other near the last step of the stairs. The Mexicans had to release their hold of the railing and step around The Second and The Third, and it was then that The Third moved and rolled, not unlike a bowling ball, and he crashed into the two Mexicans, bringing them down together. The three men rolled around on the floor looking like a rugby scrimmage. It was two against one, but the long shot for The Third was that the suddenness of the movement and the element of surprise would allow him to take out both younger men. The Mexicans were momentarily at a disadvantage, and it appeared that the older man just might pull it off. However, the Mexicans also had the youth advantage, meaning they could move faster, and that was the key. The Third stood up but did not move fast enough, and while he had succeeded in knocking down the two men, he had not succeeded in stopping them. Within a heartbeat, The Third was once again tied up and lying down on the basement floor next to his father.

Up to this time the Mexican men had looked upon the father and son and the other two hostages as a kind of annoyance factor that went along with the assignment. But now they were both angry, and it was all they could do to not shoot all four then and there. They were not entirely stupid, just mad, but they did realize that cooler heads must prevail. They were more scared of their handlers back in Mexico, and so they wisely decided to put some space between the four hostages and themselves. They retied The Third with extra tight knots, and not being very gentle, they checked the other three people, letting them know they were in control. The message was loud and clear as the Mexicans climbed the stairs to Lenny's house, and they turned off the overhead bulb plunging the basement into darkness.

The creaking of the door only emphasized the silence in the basement. The Second was still unconscious, and Lenny and Allie both had their ropes and handkerchiefs over their mouths tightened, and so The Third was the first one to speak in a whisper. "They'll be back soon," he said, "and we must be ready for them. I just need to figure out how."

The Mexicans were only working with each other because that was the way this assignment had gone. Each man would have preferred to be working as a loner and gone their own way, but they realized that when on certain assignments, one had to work within whatever circumstance presented itself. Still, neither was too bright, and instead of giving themselves a few hours to sleep or form a plan, they moved ahead. They had both tried, separately, to contact their Mexican handlers, but neither man could get through, which only made them more anxious. They checked the security of the house, making sure the windows inside and out were secure, and they locked any outside doors. Once back into the kitchen, they checked their guns and pooled their ammunition and decided they should make a move. After all, they thought, they had four people tied up, and they should act while they could. So they positioned themselves at the top of the stairs, and on a silent count, they threw open the door and moved down the basement stairs. They had not accounted for the darkness, which slowed them down, and in silence they marched down the stairs. They reached up and pulled the cord that hung from the single light bulb in the ceiling, and shadows and shards of light bounced off the walls, making their vision even more offended and useless.

Still, it was now a matter of fight or flight, and just as they were about to drag The Second and The Third over into the corner with Allie and Lenny, a blinding white light appeared in the basement, blinking on and off along with the deafening sounds of horns and loud music, giving the entire basement the atmosphere of total confusion. The Mexican men were trying to grab in the direction of the hostages, but the confusion of the strobe lighting caused them to find only emptiness, and they stumbled forward, losing their balance. A body flew out of the dark shadows and pinned down one Mexican while the other man flailed in the darkness.

The horns and music and blinking lights made it impossible to know what was happening.

CHAPTER 67

My Name Is Allie

Then a voice broke through the blackness and noise, and it was Blake. He had been able to talk one of the townspeople into letting him use their car. Blake had parked out front of Lenny's house, waiting for instructions from the U.S. Special Assignments Department. When he realized that the two Mexicans had trapped the father and son and Lenny and Allie, Blake had moved into the upstairs section of the house, bringing with him a strobe light unit and a company cell phone programmed with loud horns and music. He had hidden in a closet off the main hallway, and when the Mexicans had come upstairs to talk about their plans for the hostages in the basement, Blake overheard their plan and realized he had to move quickly.

As the Mexicans went down the basement stairs to shoot the four hostages, it was time for Blake to choose and make his move. He did succeed in that he was able to blindside one of the Mexicans who fell down the stairs, twisting his foot and knee so that he could not move. However, the other Mexican was in the right place at the right time to find a way to get behind Blake, and he jammed his gun into Blake's ribs and told him to turn off the lights and the sound, or it would be the last thing he remembered.

Blake did as he was told, and the house and basement plunged into silence and darkness. A man's brusque voice with a Mexican accent filled the void as he said, "I have my gun in the back of someone, and I can easily pull the trigger if I do not get complete control of this area. I am going to turn on the basement light, and no one is to move or speak." He added, "And you, the one I have my gun rammed in your ribs, you speak out and tell your friends to do as I say. And do it NOW!" He yelled for emphasis, and so Blake spoke and quietly said, "Do as he says. Speak up. He does have a gun, and I am sure he will use it."

Allie was the first to speak. She said, "My name is Allie." Lenny followed giving his name, and finally The Third spoke identifying himself and saying that his father was unconscious and could not speak. The Mexican who had twisted his knee was the last to speak, and he only said, "I cannot move." The only person who was not tied up or unconscious was Blake. The Mexican who had the gun in Blake's back pushed it even harder and that was a mistake as Blake physically reacted and immediately twisted to the side, surprising and throwing the Mexican with the gun off balance. Blake was still holding the strobe light and the cell phone programmed with all the noise, and he immediately turned both back on. He had the advantage of knowing this would happen, and he easily fell on the Mexican with the gun and pulled it out of his hands. He raised the heavy strobe light over his head and brought it down as hard as he could on the head of the Mexican, knocking him unconscious.

And so it was that both the Mexican cartel handlers were out of commission.

CHAPTER 68

I Am David

Blake took a moment to get his strength back, and the strobe light and the noisy cell phone were both still going full force.

Allie started to cry, and Lenny was also on the verge of breaking up. The Second was moaning as he was coming out of his unconscious state, and it was only The Third who spoke, and very much out of character, he started to swear and yell that he had been responsible for it all, and it was his fault. He had not been able to see that Blake had knocked out the second Mexican man, so he thought they were all still in danger, so he just yelled and yelled.

Suddenly, the noise and the lights stopped, and through the silence, a small voice spoke up and cut through the air.

"I am David," it said. "I am David, and I am here to get the vial and I want to talk to Sir." You could hear a pin drop; the silence was so overpowering, and then The Third found his voice and softly said, "David? David, is that really you?"

Blake turned on the single overhead light in the basement and said, "David, you made it in time, and I am so proud of you. I called the intelligence office, and I was hoping they would find you."

David said, "The nice man from the government office brought me here so I can give the vial to Sir. It belongs to him." No one spoke, and then The Third let out a chuckle and then another and soon he was hysterically laughing. Blake moved swiftly to untie Allie, Lenny, The Second, and The Third. Then Blake and The Third securely tied up both Mexican men. By this time, The Second had regained consciousness, and the Third helped his father to stand. Together, everyone made their way up the basement stairs with The Third gently escorting his father. When everyone was safely upstairs, The Third began to speak.

"This has all been my fault," he said, "and I am so sorry that you all have had to become involved as it's been." He paused. "It has been more than hectic."

"Hectic is putting it mildly," said Lenny. "And I hope you will make it up to each of these folks that you have severely inconvenienced like buying everyone a good meal, but…" and he chuckled. "I have to say that part of the adventure definitely was exciting." The Third went on, and he introduced Freedman Carver II as his father. The Third explained that he was the scientist who had developed a serum that hugely advanced seed growth and development and that, if handled correctly, could possibly solve the problem of global starvation.

He introduced his lifelong friend, Lenny, who, by way of a fall in his home, had suffered a bout of amnesia and how he and Lenny ran a small laboratory in Lenny's home. He explained that Allie was an employee from the retirement home Whispering Palms where The Third lived. He said that the two Mexican men were members of the Mexican cartel anxious to steal the vial with the serum for their home country. The Third said he knew that the Mexicans were following him, and so he had asked Allie if she would consider making the trip to give the vial to his friend Lenny. The Third paused again and expressed his apologies for all that had happened.

Suddenly, Lenny raised his voice and said, "Well, go on and tell us the whole story. Who is Blake? And who is David?"

The Third said, "Well, the two of them are like a final chapter in this story. Blake works for the United States Intelligence Commission and, unbeknownst to me, had been assigned to follow me because I once used a U.S. laboratory to provide a double-blind study of the serum. That is how they were aware of the serum and its possible potential."

The Third continued. I asked Allie, who is an activities director at Whispering Palms to take the serum to Lenny at his home, and while she was doing that, Blake moved in and befriended her. Blake was also following whoever had the vial, and that was Allie."

Allie spoke up with a small, quiet voice and said, "So then Blake was only using me because I had the vial?"

Blake said, "No, Allie. It was not like that at all. I was assigned to follow you by the United States government, and I found that I really enjoyed your company, but I also had to do my job, and that was to follow you as you had possession of the vial."

"So how does David fit in?" said Allie.

The Third said, "David is a longtime friend of mine, Allie. I knew him when I was a young scientist, and David was a delivery boy who brought me my weekly order of groceries. When I realized that the Mexican cartel was following me, I asked David if he would be able to keep a vial for me until I needed it, and he said he would."

David spoke up. "And Sir and I are friends, and he sent people to bring me here. I like him, and he likes me."

Lenny's memory was quickly returning, and he was remembering more about his friend, The Third. The Second had a small concussion but would eventually recover, and Allie and Blake stood very close to each other, holding hands, each feeling that they may have met that someone who would someday be very special in their lives.

Lenny said, "Freedman, I would never in a million years have thought you were this complicated to have connections with the United States Intelligence Office and the Mexican cartel and a nice girl like Allie and a sweet boy like David, and all of it because of the serum you put in a vial."

The Third said, "Lenny, it may seem like that, but I am just a lone scientist who happened to be successful with an experiment and who found a few friends to help with its transportation. The vial is here now, and it is safe with me, and I personally thank each person for their part in this adventure."

And as the group mingled and got ready to go out for dinner, The Third quietly slipped the vial of life into his satchel so that it would safely stay with him until it went to the laboratory that he shared with Lenny.

There would be a time to share the contents of the vial with the world, but that time was not now. Now was the time for a few friends who had been drawn together through their association with an obscure scientist who went by the name of The Third and their mutual desires to protect the vial and its contents. Now was the time to celebrate and enjoy dinner and each other. And so, they did just that.

ABOUT THE AUTHOR

Marilyn cannot remember a time when she was not writing. Canadian born, she attended the Studio of Theatrical Arts in Victoria, British Columbia, training in theater arts. She was a flight attendant at Pacific Western Airline when she met and married a producer, Dudley Remus. They traveled the United States for twenty years producing outdoor spectaculars with Marilyn directing and writing the scripts for the shows. They settled in Longview, Texas, where Marilyn established the Studio of Creative Arts. After a divorce, she raised her son, Wayne, using her stenographic skills to support them while working for a cable company; and she established, hosted, and wrote for a television show called *Around the Town.* Marilyn returned to Canada to be near her family, and she resides in New Westminster, British Columbia, with her cat, Cinnamon. *The Vial of Life* is her first full-length novel. She continues to write.

ACKNOWLEDGEMENTS

This novel has been over thirty years in its inception.

I am grateful to my parents, Mary and Joseph Sommers, who always allowed me the freedom to write from my imagination.

My #1 son and his Florida family gave me support bordering on unbelievable generosity and close friends, Jo-Anne Pearce and Maria Uher, who offered their solid support during the long hours and difficult task of final editing. I am ever-grateful to the ChristianFaithPublishing Company for their approval and assistance in publication.

May you share this story with others for their enjoyment of my novel, "The Vial of Life".

Marilyn Remus, Author

"The Vial of Life